WILD WOLF'S TWISTED TAILS

An anthology of dark tales from the acclaimed Wild Wolf stable of writers

A Wild Wolf Publication

Published by Wild Wolf Publishing in 2014

Copyright © 2014 Wild Wolf Publishing and the respected authors

First print

ISBN: 978-1-907954-24-5

Also available in e-book

www.wildwolfpublishing.com

PRAISE FOR WILD WOLF AUTHORS

"Compelling and disturbing in equal measure.'
~ The Guardian

"One the most heart racing, jaw-dropping novels that I have ever dared to finish."
~ The Crack Magazine

"...enchanting."
~ The Skinny

"Compelling and intense."
~ Liz Williams

"A truly chilling novel."
~ Borders Books

"An exploration of pure evil."
~ Remotegoat.co.uk

"Compelling and disturbing."
~ Melrose Books

"...dazzled ... lushly textured, with each page bearing an exquisitely crafted turn of phrase."
--Christopher Brookmyre

"Darkly imaginative."
~ Discovered Authors

"Genuinely creepy."
~ Light Up Glasgow's Skyline

"Tightly written piece of noir fiction."
~ HarperCollins

Thank you, oh dark and wondrous wielder of the magical pen.

FOREWORD

Wild Wolf Publishing was set up in 2007 by several like-minded individuals with the belief that mainstream publishing was largely ignoring new talent, especially at the darker end of the literary spectrum. We decided to get off our backsides and do something about it. And so, Wild Wolf Publishing was born and submissions opened for darker, edgier fiction.

Six years later, we have published over 60 titles in both print and e-book formats. We have had several best-sellers and have won a number of awards and critical acclaim.

This anthology is a showcase for many of our authors. At the end of each story, you will find links to more titles by that author. If you enjoy the story, please do consider reading more of their work. All of our titles cost less than a cup of coffee, so go on give them a try.

Thank you to the readers for taking chances with new and emerging authors and thank you to the authors for their skill and imagination and for never giving up the dream. And for being as twisted as the Wild Wolf team!

Wild Wolf Publishing

Fiction ... with TEETH.

www.wildwolfpublishing.com

CONTENTS

GABBY

By Rod Glenn

A clock ticks.

The man groans and pushes the duvet from his face. His bloodshot eyes blink several times as he stares up at the ceiling. Sunshine squeezes through a narrow gap in the curtains.

The blood on his face has dried and is caked into his stubble. He pulls his hand out from under the covers and winces in pain. Frowning, he stares at it. It too is smeared with blood and his knuckles are torn and scabbed.

With that action, suddenly the rest of his body screams for attention.

"What the ..." Words fail him as he clambers out of bed, wincing and groaning with every little motion.

He stands and looks down at his ravaged body. He is drenched in dried blood, scratches, scrapes and bruises. Despite his own extensive injuries, he is acutely aware that not all of the blood can be his. There's far too much of it.

His sheets and duvet are covered and there are bloody smears across the laminate floor to the door.

He begins to tremble uncontrollably. "What the fuck?" he repeats to himself over and over, hugging himself.

"Gabby?" he calls out. "*Gabby!*" The second time is shrill, his voice cracking.

He staggers towards the door, wincing and gripping his swollen knee. The landing is in darkness, the curtains still closed. He shoves open the door to the spare room. Empty. The bathroom. Empty.

He catches a glimpse of his crimson face in the mirror.

"Gabby!"

Ignoring the protests from his body, he thunders down the stairs three at a time and kicks open the door to the lounge and dining room. Deserted. He stumbles into the kitchen, sweating and tears streaming down his face.

A young petite red headed woman is standing by the cooker, frying eggs, humming to herself absently. As he staggers into the room, she glances over to him and smiles. Her porcelain skin is peppered with tiny freckles that at first appear to be spots of blood.

"Hi, sweetheart," she says. "Breakfast is nearly ready. Bacon and eggs for my baby."

He stares at her, mouth agape. "What ... happened?" He thrusts his arms out and gestures to his blood-stained body.

Gabby giggles. "Oh, silly, you tried to stop me again."

Confusion sets into his features. "What? I ... I don't understand."

She sighs and begins plating up two breakfasts. "You took a bit of a knock, sweetheart. I had to put you to bed. It'll come back to you."

He grabs the kitchen table to steady himself. "A bit of a knock? I'm covered in blood!"

As she places the plates on the table, she says, "Don't worry, silly, most of it isn't yours."

"Most of it! Whose is it?"

"Come on, sweetheart, eat your breakfast before it gets cold."

Anger slices through his confusion. "Gabby, what the fuck happened?"

She sighs again and there's genuine sorrow behind her bright emerald eyes. "You followed me. I warned you not to. You tried to stop me claim my kill. You know what I get like. She was a pretty little thing – just your type."

His eyes grew wide. "My God, Gabby, what have you done?"

She was looking down at her plate, her red hair falling around her face. She remained like that for a time, still, silent.

He couldn't take it any longer. He slammed a fist onto the table, jolting the cutlery. "Gabby!"

Suddenly, she sprung to her feet and pinned him against the worktop. Those piercing green eyes burned into his soul and, in a low guttural growl, she uttered, "It was my time of the month ... *sweetheart*."

THE END

Further titles by Rod Glenn

STORMY WEATHER

By Jo Reed

Henry was getting close. Karen could tell by the scent of ozone on the wind, the prickling static on her skin. A raindrop the size of a quail's egg exploded on her cheek. Then another. She didn't bother to duck as overhanging branches whipped across her face, but forced herself upright and ran, diving down familiar narrow pathways, deeper into the maze of Puzzle Wood. Tears blurred the path as she pitched round the next turn, made for the fragile bridge, the storm coming on behind.

It hadn't always been like this. There was a time when Henry's smile made her knees quiver, when his voice made her catch her breath. There were days when Henry made the snow, the sun, the rain, just for her.

The day they met, she wasn't in the mood for company. She sat, oozing misery into an espresso double shot. He walked into the coffee shop, ordered Chinese tea and sat at the next table. 'Won't help,' he said. 'Too much caffeine in that stuff.'

She looked up. Henry was smiling. He glowed as if a sudden shaft of light had come through the window behind him, except it was November and the only thing outside was thick fog. His blond hair glinted, blue eyes held her, but it was the smile that caught her, reaching out like a silk cord, twining, tugging. A slight breeze stirred her long chestnut hair, a strand floating across her face as if he had stroked her cheek.

'Yeah,' she said. 'I guess you're right.'

'I'm Henry. Would you like some tea instead? I think there's enough here to last me a week. I can ask for another cup – no problem.'

'Karen,' she said, and joined him.

They talked. At some point they exchanged phone numbers. As he left, the fog cleared.

Next day, Henry called. She realised how nice his voice sounded without the distraction of the smile. As he talked she felt a cool finger of air run down her spine, a sudden draft from the gap underneath the door.

'No,' she said, 'I really don't feel like going out tonight. But if you'd like to come over …'

Ten minutes later she was at the front door, looking at Henry's smile.

'I hate this weather!' she said, after spaghetti with green pesto and red wine, lying with Henry on the rug.

Henry glanced at the window, the steady drizzle pattering against the panes. 'So what kind of weather would you like?' He was smiling again.

'Winter is for snow,' she said. 'Snow, and a log fire, mulled wine and chestnuts. Don't you think?'

Henry laughed. His mouth was close to her ear when he whispered, 'Look out of the window.'

She saw nothing so he pulled her up, turned off the light. They stood, holding hands, watching snowflakes gather on the sill.

Next morning, Karen woke thinking of Henry. Just after midday the doorbell rang. Henry carried a bunch of flowers so big she couldn't see his smile until he parted the stems with his fingers. 'Where would you like to go?' he said.

'Somewhere warm,' she answered, pulling her shawl closer, 'but I'll settle for a walk in Puzzle Wood.'

Henry waited while she found an extra sweater to put on under her overcoat and wound a long scarf twice round her neck.

'I'll never find you under all that!' he said, grabbing her round the waist and kissing her. 'You never know.' He winked. 'Might snow tonight.'

They walked through the winding pathways, sliding on damp leaf litter, until Henry confessed he was lost.

'Don't worry,' she said. 'I've known this wood since I was a child. You won't get lost as long as you're with me. I promise.'

His smile faded and, for the first time, he looked serious. 'I wish I could be with you forever,' he whispered. 'Stay with me. Belong to me — always.'

'I love you, Henry,' she said.

Henry sat back, studying her. At last he grinned, eyes twinkling, and said, 'Want to know a secret?'

She nodded.

'Promise you won't be afraid.' He was stroking the hair away from her face with reticent fingers, trembling a little, although it might have been the cold.

'I won't be afraid,' she said, taking his hand.

'Okay. You said you wanted to be somewhere warm?'

Henry pulled her to her feet and held her still. He closed his eyes, his breath misting against her skin. The clouds above them parted. The sun, beating down, blazed hot on her damp hair, made the ground steam, curled the leaves at her feet. Henry took off his coat, then his sweater and threw them down, laughing. Just along the path she could see the rain, still falling hard, striking the branches, making them shudder. But where they stood the sun burned her face. She was sweating under the coat.

'Henry?'

'Take off your scarf, you'll fry in there!'

'But, Henry…' She felt the blood draining from her cheeks. Then she was falling, her vision fading until only the twinkle of his eyes remained.

When she came round he was taking off her scarf, her coat, and she was propped up, her back against a tree. He was bare-chested, sunbathing, a pair of Raybans hiding his eyes, but not his smile.

'For you, Karen,' he said. 'Sunshine for the woman I love.'

Karen tried to hide her fear, but Henry's face darkened. 'You promised. You said you loved me. You promised you wouldn't be afraid.'

Karen saw a tear roll from beneath the Raybans. At the same time the sky clouded and it started to rain. Her fear was tinged with shame. 'Henry, I'm sorry. I love you. I'm not afraid.'

Karen couldn't remember exactly when Henry moved into her flat. It might have been a week, or two. He came with nothing but a change of clothes and a box of handmade chocolates. One of the chocolates was missing, in its place a ring, platinum and set with an emerald to match her eyes. Later, he stopped the rain to let the moon shine through the window.

On Christmas morning he gave her snow, roasted chestnuts and made mulled wine. When she looked out of the window she saw that the fall stopped halfway down the street, the rest bathed in weak winter sun. A few people were outside, pointing, their mouths wide. Henry winked and made it rain, the snow dissolving to nothing by the time anyone thought to take a photograph. On New Year 's Day they drove to the coast and had a summer picnic with champagne, hidden in a deserted cove.

Wherever Karen went, Henry went too. He took her to the supermarket, walked with her to the post box, even to the hairdresser, waiting inside or by the window in the café opposite. Every morning she woke to find him sitting, watching her, a tray of tea and toast beside the bed. As soon as she opened her eyes he pulled back the curtains to let in streaming sunlight, whatever the natural climate was doing.

'Sunshine for the woman I love.'

By the end of winter, Karen felt that perhaps it would be nice to wake up to rain. She told Henry she would like to go out by herself now and then. He frowned, and the flat was filled with a biting wind, pushing her away from the door, great ice patterns forming on the windows so she couldn't see out. She could do nothing but kiss him and draw him back to bed. The only way to feel safe was to make him smile. From that moment she wished she could open her eyes in the morning and not see Henry.

When she told Henry she'd like to go out to work, his smile disappeared.

'Without me? You can't go anywhere without me. You promised. You said you would stay with me forever. You belong to me – always.'

The sky was suddenly dark. She heard the wind howling, battering on the window panes. 'Henry! Stop it! You can't do this, you have to stop!' She was shouting to make herself heard above the wind. Then came a flash of lightning, the sound of shattering glass and a great roll of thunder overhead. The curtains, snapping in the gale, tore loose from the rail. A wine bottle crashed from the table. Another lightening bolt, so close she could smell the burning, lanced down onto her car on the road below. More breaking glass, more thunder. 'I won't go. I won't go anywhere, I promise, just stop this, stop it now!'

The room was still, just a faint pattering of rain dying away in the silence.

'Stay with me, Karen. I'm lost without you.'

'It's all right, Henry,' she said, reaching out a shaking hand. 'I won't go.'

Henry smiled and put his arms around her. 'I love you, Karen. Let's go somewhere warm.'

After a while, Karen stopped wondering if the weather was real, or what Henry created. He put locks on all the doors and windows so they would be safe while he slept. He kept the key on a chain around his neck. One afternoon, when he was in the shower, she broke the window and tried to climb out. The storm came before she had the chance to jump down onto the shed roof, two storeys below. Henry finished his shower

16

while she stayed, huddled on the sill, watching lightning set the shed ablaze, the felt roof shimmering blue like St. Elmo's fire.

When Henry came out of the bathroom and helped her back inside, he said, 'You can't leave me, Karen. You can never leave me. I won't let you go. I'd be lost without you.'

She pressed against him, holding him until he smiled. 'Do you remember the first time you took me out?' she said. 'You made the sun shine, just for me.'

He kissed her. 'I remember.'

'Let's go out together. Let's go to Puzzle Wood and walk in the sunshine, just like we did that day.'

Henry shook his head. Karen said nothing. Each morning when he showed her his sunshine she laughed and hugged him close. During the days she followed him round the flat, chatting, standing beside him, joining him in the shower. On the next shopping trip she put Chinese tea into the basket and bought a large teapot with a bamboo handle. That afternoon she made tea, and told him how much she loved him.

'Tomorrow,' Henry said, 'we should go to Puzzle Wood.'

It was a sunny day, hot enough for June, Karen thought. They walked along the paths, deep into the wood, and stopped for a picnic under the trees. As Henry turned to pack the things away she crept, heart racing, until she got through the trees and onto the next path. She knew the maze better than anyone. Henry didn't.

When she got to the path she started to run, up the hill towards the footbridge spanning Wyndham Gully, over the ancient, dried up river bed two hundred feet below. She heard Henry call out twice and kept on running. She saw clouds gathering, felt the wind whipping up behind her as Henry began to move.

The woodland fell away and she was in the open, running onto the narrow wooden bridge, the structure creaking and swinging in Henry's gale. She stumbled almost to the far side and stopped, chest heaving, knees trembling with fatigue. It was perhaps five seconds, no longer, and Henry came clear of the trees. The storm raged around him, the fury in his eyes sparked by lightning flashes as he stepped onto the bridge, gripped the handrails to stop himself from falling. She saw his mouth shape her name, barely caught the words that followed; 'I won't let you go!'

Karen stood still. Henry, and the storm, came on. He was in the middle of the bridge. The air around them crackled, so thin she couldn't take a breath. For a split second the sky glowed blue, then the charge was released in a great flash, snaking down towards her. She threw herself backwards, off the bridge and onto bare earth. The bolt struck the spot where she had been standing, its tendrils shooting along the metal sheaths that covered the handrails, incinerating the wood underneath.

She saw the moment the lightning reached Henry. It all happened with a strange grace, as if time had stretched each second into ten. He seemed to rise up, his body a blue-red flame against the dark sky. Above the clamour of the storm she thought she heard a final cry; 'Don't leave me!' Then the bridge disintegrated, plunged, flaming, onto the rocks far below.

The wind died. The clouds parted; the clearing was bathed in sunshine. Somewhere, deep in the woodland, Karen heard the faint tapping of a green woodpecker. It was going to be a warm afternoon.

THE END

Further titles by Jo Reed

The Tyranny of the Blood
A Child of the Blood
Malim's Legacy

THE VOICE

By Kevin Tomsett

I can feel myself slowly slipping, slipping back into the old ways; the voices are starting to talk to me, those same voices I thought I had silenced over a year ago. They tell me what I have to do, I have to kill again. The voices are calling louder now, it's almost deafening. "Pick up the knife, pick up the knife..." they keep saying. "NO!" I scream, "Not again..." I run into the kitchen and there on the side is a butcher's knife glinting in the moonlight, just begging me to pick it up. "Do it, do it, you know you want to, you need to, you have to."

I pick up the knife and look at the reflection but don't recognise the face I see staring back at me, the face grins at me, "You know what to do, and you know how to do it." I now feel like a stranger inside my own body, I turn and leave my kitchen and walk down the hall and out of my front door. The street is deserted as I walk down it and turn the corner; a woman is standing, leaning against a lamppost looking like a cheap whore. She is wearing a micro skirt and a skimpy top, showing off her big boobs and talking on her phone. I lift the knife and walk up behind her placing one hand around her mouth and guiding the knife up to her throat. The blade sinks deep into her flesh like a hot knife into butter; her blood gushes from her neck, she chokes and falls silent. She drops to the ground as the blood pools around her and trickles over the edge of the curb. The rush of adrenalin courses through my body and I like the feeling and I need more.

The next morning I was awoken by the local news on the radio, "….and in local news a young girl was brutally murdered last night after she was attacked whilst waiting for a bus at Victoria Woodholme car park in Buckfastleigh; local police are appealing for witnesses."

I look around my bedroom in horror, what happened last night, was that me? The last thing I remember is…oh no the kitchen! I jump out of bed and race into the kitchen looking over at the knife block I notice that the butcher's knife is missing. I start to panic. Where could it be? I look all around the kitchen in cupboards, as well as in the bin but nothing. I stand stock still and look around the room, the sink! I slowly walk over to it and there, sure enough is the knife covered in blood. I start to feel sick as I stagger back in horror and bump into the kitchen table. The doorbell rings and I try to compose myself as I hurry to the door, I notice that, unusually, the chain is across the door. I decide to leave it there and open the door very slowly. "Good morning sir" booms a voice from the other side. It's the police! I start to panic again "Can I help you?" I answer, looking at the man's badge "A young lady was murdered last night and we are canvassing the area to find out if anyone has heard or seen anything." Every bone in my body is shaking as I try so hard to keep my cool; I am surprised the policeman can't hear my knees knocking. "No sorry I didn't as I was sleeping and I've only just got up." I don't think he bought what I said. "Ok sir but if you do remember anything please do give us a call." He hands me his card, I smile and close the door. I then roll around to the wall and sink to my knees with my head in my hands. This can't be happening, not to me. I look back toward the kitchen; this has to be a bad dream. I slowly walk back into the kitchen and up to the sink. The knife is still there, seemingly taunting me. "It's no dream!" How can I clean off the blood? I start biting my nails, and then it suddenly dawns on me. The dishwasher! I'd seen it in an episode of Crime Scene Investigation where a normal knife was found in a dishwasher and there was no trace of what had happened, no DNA, nothing. I quickly fill the drawers with the washing up and the knife and set the program to boil. The blood in the sink comes off easily with help from a cupboard full of cleaning chemicals.

I sit at my kitchen table and stare at the knife block with its missing knife and try to recall the events of last night. Why was the knife on the table and not in the block, why can't I remember? The entire night is a blank; did I really kill that young girl? Am I capable of doing such things? As the questions went round and round my head, I came to the conclusion that I'm part of someone's sick game and left it at that and went on with my day.

An hour passed and the dishwasher finished its cycle, so I open the door and take out the knife and place it back into the block. "It was you, you know." Comes a voice from the hallway "Hello!" I shout like the fool I am "You killed that girl last night, with my help." the voice says again. I walk over to the kitchen door and look down the hallway to the front door but no one is there. "Ok now I must be going mad I'm hearing voices." Just as I am about to turn away the voice screams at me, "DON'T YOU WALK AWAY FROM ME!" I freeze on the spot and a cold shiver runs down my spine, I start to panic and fumble in my pocket for my inhaler, my chest constricting painfully. I start to walk down my hallway as slowly as I can; I peer around the corner of the front room, nothing there. I move to the bottom of the stairs and look up again, no one there. Where is this voice coming from? I look at my reflection in the hall mirror and shake my head. "Now I know I'm going crazy!" I say to myself. "No you're not!" My reflection says as it walks towards me. "You did it you did it all!!" It taunts me as I am frozen with fear. Can this be possible, can a reflection talk? "Yes" it says again. "I can talk and yes I'm real, well as real as you have made me." It knows what I'm thinking but how? "I can hear your thoughts because I am you, haven't you figured this out yet you stupid little man?" I puff on my inhaler in abject fear. "I've seen too many films to know that if I start hearing voices then I've gone mad or insane!" I say to this person that stands in my mirror, "But I have always been in your head waiting for the right time." What does he mean the right time? "Look in your basement." The voice instructs me, and I look around to the door behind me. "Go on down you go." I open the door, turn on the light and slowly proceed down the stairs. I gasp in horror as I see a woman sitting bound and gagged to a chair, but I can't make out her face from where I'm standing so I move closer and closer until I'm standing in front of her. She looks up at me with tears in her eye, I gasp and stumble back. "You!" I shout "What the FUCK are you doing here?" She tries to scream at me but the gag in her mouth muffles the sound. "Ah so you do remember her, so you also remember the day she tried to run you over in her car." Anger filled every fibre in my body as I relived that day again in my mind. "It was on that day that I was born and I grew with all the lies that she spread to all your school friends, she made your young adult life a living hell." The voice continued to taunt me. Anger and hate have started to consume me now as I walk up to her and punch her as hard as I can in her fat face. Her and the chair fall backwards; I pick her and the chair up and look at her face. I have broken her nose, that makes me feel good but not good enough. I look around the basement and spy a lump of wood, I pick it up and run at her. I swing it behind me and let it fly towards her once again it catches her in her ear and splinters fly into her eye. Now I feel better! I beat her many more times around the head as she falls silent. I check her pulse, she is alive but just barely. It's time now to finish her and free myself from her lies for ever. I walk back upstairs and into my study, pick up my gun from my desk drawer and walk back down to the basement. She hasn't moved so I walk up to her, point the gun at the back of her head and pull the trigger. I watch impassively as her brains explode from the front of her skull and a feeling of relief washes over me. I can finally lay this ghost to rest….but now I have fed the voice and I must continue to kill.

COOKING WITHOUT ONIONS

By CW Lovatt

"So, I'll see you tomorrow?"

"Absolutely," then, lightly cajoling, I lie, "you know that you can count on me."

I can hear her giggle on the other end of the line. "I can't wait."

My mind screams, *Tell her, you fool! Why don't you just open your mouth and say it?*

In fact, my mouth does open.

She asks, "What was that?"

'Tell her!

Then it closes again.

"Nothing, just clearing my throat."

"Okay!" She's over the moon. "Well, there's a lot to get ready, so I guess I'd better go."

"Okay."

"Oh, and hon…?"

I hate it when she calls me that. It sounds comfortable and relaxed, and yes…it sounds safe. She shouldn't feel safe – no, not at all.

"Yeah?"

"I love you so much."

I can see her in my imagination without any difficulty, looking all emotional, like she's got a bad case of gas, and I find myself struggling with a strong surge of anger that has no base in reason. But that's okay, reason's a commodity that I seldom have a use for anyway.

She waits, expecting a reply.

I swallow hard and mutter, "Love you too."

Christ, the words taste like hemlock, making me grimace.

She laughs, "You men! You're always so hopeless when it comes to saying what's in your heart."

Wasn't that just the truth, the whole truth, and nothing but the truth?

"Yeah well," I continue to mumble, "guess I'd better let you go."

"All right, see you tomorrow."

"Uh huh."

"Bye!"

"Bye."

I hang up the phone and make straight for the liquor cabinet. The first shot goes down like water, so does the second. By the time the third is chasing after them, it's finally starting to burn. When the fourth is safely inside, I'm beginning to feel Grade 'A' bonafide pissed, so I think, why stop now?

I'm so centered on my mission that I toss the glass aside and tip the bottle to my lips, feeling the fire coursing through my body, feeding my anger until it's not possible to feel anything else.

The danger is that this procedure can also get me affectionately maudlin, or more often than not, reeling drunk and full of self-loathing. The worst of it is that the courage that's supposed to come with it seldom bothers to materialize. God if only it did, then it still might be okay! I'd just call her up and tell her to forget about me. I wouldn't even bother with that other claptrap about wanting to remain friends, or anything like that; just a simple merciless blow. After all, that would be better than the alternative, I'm sure.

But I'm not much of a one for courage — artificial or otherwise. I hate that about myself, so it follows that I loath her for not hating me, too, the stupid bitch! Part of me wants her to run away - to save herself - but another, darker part wants to punish her for wanting to save *me* - for allowing herself to fall in love with someone who will never be able to return the favour, but at the same time is too afraid to let her go.

And how did that come about? Was something lacking in my genes, or had it become entrenched over the years? Whatever the reason, I know that in order to savour life to the fullest, you have to have the strength to steer your own course, but knowing about it is as far as I'll ever get; and in a way, *knowing* about it makes it even worse. It's a hell of a thing being afraid — too afraid to live, or even, when you get right down to it, too afraid to die.

Just once I'd like to see it in her eyes — the fear - to know what it's like to feel the way I feel every day. Maybe once will be all that I'll ever need. Maybe once will be all that she'll ever get.

But she's not afraid. Right at this moment she's happily engrossed, preparing for our wedding tomorrow. We're going to tie the knot, to take that first step past the point of no return. This, as in virtually everything else, from our first date on up to the present, is her idea, not mine. But now the time is approaching, I know that it's going to be the biggest mistake of our lives. Just as I know I'm going to go ahead with it all the same. Because, like it or not, I also know that I'd reached that point of no return long ago; probably before I ever met her.

Through the booze fumes I see it all laid out in front of me, all of the rest of my life. Without the courage to seek my own way, I will never experience what is supposed to be part and parcel to that. Without it, my journey towards the abyss will lack the vital essence of flavour. It will be like eating from a dish that has been distilled of taste – just a gruel of indifference - when all around me there will be the aromas of banquets fit for kings. One thing is certain: whatever the cards hold in store, living a lie guarantees that happiness is never going to play a part in it. That's what she was stealing from me! She was sacrificing my happiness for her own, and I just didn't have the substance to stand in her way! The mere thought makes me so angry that I could…that I could just…I don't know! I just don't know how far I will go, but I do know that at some point we're going to find out.

No, she's not afraid…but she will be!

THE END

Further titles by CW Lovatt

The Adventures of Charlie Smithers
Josiah Stubb: The Siege of Louisbourg

KLINGSOR'S FIRST SUMMER

By N A Randall

The transit van pulled up to the side of the road. A man with ginger hair leaned out of the passenger window, and glared at me with mad, piercing blue eyes.

I quickly looked away.

The gang-master got out of the driver's side. I could tell he was disappointed I wasn't a strapping six-footer who would be of some practical use to him that summer. Regardless, he shook my hand and welcomed me aboard.

'Oh, and don't worry 'bout Deano.' He gestured towards the passenger window. 'He's like that with everyone.'

As soon as I opened the door the smell hit me: twelve semi-conscious men still stinking of their beds and last night's booze. I clambered in and tried to sleep, but Deano's incessant chatter proved too distracting. Every so often, one of the men farted and he would shout, 'I smell sperm, I smell sperm,' then laugh himself silly.

The drive lasted nearly two hours.

Once out of the van, I followed after the other men, trudging along with their heads hanging low, coughing and hawking. Everyone looked so weary, despite the fact the working day had yet to begin.

There was a half-mile trek across a desolate stretch of farm land. The early morning sunshine felt hot and oppressive. But it was the silence, an ominous quiet that struck me most. Even the birds seemed to make no sound.

When we got to the field the gang-master took me and a lad called Dimitri to one side. Handing us each a pair of rubber gloves, he explained that as we were the youngest we were going to be "riddling." I had no idea what he meant.

We climbed onto a covered trailer attached to a tractor, and stood either side of a mechanical conveyor belt. As the tractor moved, so did the belt, and on it, the potatoes. Spotted amongst the rolling harvest were all types of things: carcasses, stones, green or rotten potatoes. It was our job to remove them. Rotten potatoes were the worst. The stench is hard to describe–dog sick or curdled milk. Just thinking about it makes me retch.

It took less than thirty minutes for the boredom to really sink in. The mind numbing repetition, being shunted this way and that, the clunking belt and tubercular engine noise, the dirt and dust, hands working furiously, more often than not failing to grab something slippery and disgusting before it fell from the belt, destined for the bottom of some unsuspecting shopping bag.

Two hours passed, maybe three. I was lost in the nothingness when the engine and belt stopped. Then I heard someone shout "tea break." It sounded like a hymn to the Lord.

I glanced across at Dimitri. The look on his face needed no words.

Just as we were about to climb down, Deano leapt onto the side of the trailer armed with a rotten potato. It whistled just past my face. Dimitri wasn't so lucky. It hit him square on the chest, exploding in a pulpy mush.

The rest of the workers were sitting in the middle of the field, smoking or drinking tea from Thermos flasks. The sun was hotter still. Nobody said a word, until Deano walked over.

'I screwed for England last night, boys,' he said, groping his crotch. 'She was a real cracker too, biggest tits I ever saw.'

The other men didn't respond, react, show any sign of interest.

'How old are you?'

Panicked, I feared Deano was talking to me. But when I looked up I saw him staring at Dimitri, who was still mopping the front of his T-shirt.

'Bet you're still a virgin, aren't yer?' said Deano. 'Yeah, this one hasn't had his cherry popped yet, boys. What'd you say about that, eh?'

He walked right up to Dimitri and pushed him to the floor.

'Oi, I'm talking to you.' Deano's eyes flashed. 'Don't you understand English? I said–'

'Boys!' It was the gang-master. 'Come on, back to work.'

That first day felt like it was never going to end. When it did, I had visions of whirling potatoes ingrained in my mind, like looking into the sun and seeing shapes flash behind your eyes.

As we walked back to the van, Deano persuaded the gang-master to let him drive home.

On the motorway it was as if he was hell-bent on killing us. Foot flat down, he took the rattling van to its limits, riding bumper to bumper, overtaking like a lunatic, whooping and hollering, honking the horn at women drivers, making lewd gestures as we sped by.

When I got home, I had a long soak in the bath, dreading tomorrow. But there was no way out of it. I needed the job. I needed the money.

Next day was the same: the long drive, the semi-comatose gang, Deano. It was hard to believe that someone so limited could like the sound of his own voice so much.

'Sunk sixteen pints of cider last night, boys.'

I switched off.

When we arrived the gang-master told us we'd be "bagging up." Again, I had no idea what he was talking about. On a concreted area outside some farm buildings, we set about transferring yesterday's harvest from trailers to brown sacks. Dimitri and I were allocated the least physical work: tying the sacks with thin metal wires. As quick as we worked, the numbers of bags that needed securing increased faster than we could get to them, until they were piled up everywhere.

Deano marched over.

'You fuckin' useless pair of cunts!' he shouted. 'All you've gotta do is tie these fuckers up.'

Grabbing a handful of wires, he shoved me aside and started fastening bags. No sooner had he fastened one and stacked it, he was onto the next.

'Look and learn,' he said. 'This is a piece of piss. Now you try.'

On reaching for a bag, I accidentally brushed against his stinking, sweaty body. It made me shudder.

'That's it,' he said, seeing my renewed efforts. 'You two had better get your thumbs out of your arses. We can't afford to carry no one.'

For a few minutes he stood watching over us. Then he crept up behind me and slashed my forearm with one of the wires.

During a break, we sat on some wooden pallets. It was muggy and close. As I put a plaster on my arm, Deano stepped in front of me, blocking out the sun.

'So, storky, you got into the swing of things yet? 'Cos I ain't fuckin' around when I say we can't be carrying no one. If you don't shape up, you'll be out.'

It didn't seem like such a bad thing.

'What're you doing here anyway? This is man's work, not little boys.'

'I'm going to college in September,' I replied. 'I'm hoping to save up some money.'

'Ooh.' He shook his head. 'Fuckin' poncey college boy, that's all we need! At least comrade cherry-popper over there knows how to put in a shift.'

27

Each day was as long and miserable as the next. Picked up at five, starting work at seven, not getting home until eight or nine in the evening, covered in shit and aches and pains.

Towards the end of the second week, the heavens opened. Rain was the best thing to happen all summer. Wet soil stopped work. The gang-master decided to wait it out, and started allocating middling tasks. Deano and some older men were told to go and pick potatoes by hand. I was told to sweep out one of the farm buildings.

'This little fucker has got the life of Riley,' said Deano. 'How come he gets all the cushy jobs, eh?'

He glared at me.

'It's gotta be done,' said the gang-master. 'And anyway, you'd be the first to complain if I asked you to sweep up.'

When I'd finished sweeping, I poked my head outside. It was still raining, and there was no sign of the rest of the gang. Taking a newspaper from someone's bag, I sat down and waited.

Half an hour later, I heard footsteps, and saw Deano rushing over. For protection against the rain, he was wearing a plastic rubbish bag with holes cut out for his head and arms. Plainly agitated, dripping wet, he steamed into the farm building.

'Look at you, you little bastard! Feet up, all warm and cosy, reading the fuckin' paper!'

For some reason I thought he was joking, and I smiled and shrugged.

'It's a piss-take,' he said. 'And you're a piss-taking cunt!'

He ripped off the plastic bag, his hands twitching, fit to strike out. He lurched forward. Thankfully, the van pulled up outside. But for that one moment, Deano had an even more horrible look in his eyes than I'd seen before. Muttering under his breath, he gave me a strange, disconcerting smile, then turned and walked away.

One afternoon we were raided by Immigration Officers. Half a dozen men dashed across the field like some crack SWAT team. Only instead of guns they held up pieces of paper. It didn't have quite the same effect.

As I was being questioned, Dimitri sprinted off. One of the Immigration Officers chased him down. I remember how upset Dimitri looked when he was led away, tears streaming down his cheeks. He told me he was sending money home to his family. His pay packet was literally feeding them and keeping a roof over their heads. What were my problems compared to his?

We never saw Dimitri again. He didn't have the appropriate papers to be working here. At the time I didn't realize what it would mean for me. Now I was the only one Deano could pick on.

That week, we moved to another field. A nightmare field. More stones than potatoes. We needed four men removing things from the belt. They took it in turns. The first thing Deano did when he climbed aboard was spit on my shoe. As the engine restarted, I tried to concentrate on my work, keeping a corner of my eye fixed firmly on him.

A little later, however, caught in a void of complete and utter boredom, something slimy was wiped across my cheek.

Deano burst out laughing.

'What was that?' I shouted.

'Don't worry,' he replied. 'Just something I scraped off the end of my cock.'

On the way home that night I sat directly behind the gang-master, Deano next to him, something crass exiting his mouth every other second.

'Going down the Mill tonight,' he said to the gang-master.

'That so.'

'Yeah. Gonna get me end away again. Tugged this cracker last week…she knew her onions, I can tell you. Gave me a blowy for about two hours.'

'Surely you'd have shot your bolt long before two hours were up,' said the gang-master.

'What'd you take me for? I never come before I've got inside.'

'But the good 'un's know what to do to yer, Deano.'

'So, it's happened to you, has it?' Deano sniggered. 'Bloody wars, boys.' He turned in his seat, flashing the rest of the gang a demented grin. 'Old matey boy here, only goes and shoots his load before he's got inside the pussy hole.'

His laughter annoyed the gang-master.

'Oh shut up, for fuck's sake, Dean! I'd be surprised if you knew the pussy from the piss hole.'

'What—?'

'I've known you for the best part of fifteen years, and I've never seen you with a woman. You still live with your mum, for Chrissakes.'

Everybody laughed. It felt good to see Deano put in his place for once. Better still, he didn't say another word for the rest of the journey.

The summer was drawing to a close. It felt beyond miraculous that I'd got anywhere close to seeing it through. We moved on to another nightmare field–stones, stones and more stones. In wilting heat, progress was slow. In the midst of the rattling noise, the dust swirling against broken rays of sun, I looked up for a moment, at the other men with sweat dripping from their dirt-caked brows, bodies bent at crooked, unnatural angles. I wondered what their dreams had been when they were children, when they were my age. How had they envisioned their lives working out? Rock stars? Millionaires? Footballers? Maybe even a cushy office job–surely not this. It was as if I was looking at the worst thing anyone could imagine for themselves.

That afternoon, the going was only getting worse when I heard a scream and shouts of "stop the engine."

We all jumped off the trailer. A gang member called Billy was trapped underneath the wheels, pinned to the soft, muddy ground. The gang-master was kneeling beside him, searching for some way to free him, muttering, 'Oh shit, oh shit.'

It was then Deano appeared.

'Don't fuckin' move him!' he shouted.

Barking out orders, he got most of us to take the weight of the trailer, while two others got either side of Billy, ready to pull him out. On the count of three, and in a split second, he was freed.

Miraculously, he only suffered minor injuries.

In the field afterwards, everyone crowded around Deano.

'Well done, Dean,' said the gang-master. 'I don't know what we'd have done without you, mate. You saved ole Billy's life.'

'Ah, fuck off, you daft cunt.'

'Nah, come on, Dean. I've seen this sort of thing happen before, seen legs and arms ripped off, men cut in two. If you hadn't kept your head, we–'

'Shut it.' Deano waved his words away. 'He can buy me a pint down the Mill later. Then we'll be quits.'

Lighting a cigarette, he stood there as everyone congratulated him, with this modest, almost shy expression on his face, like he didn't know how to take a compliment, a simple expression of human gratitude. At that moment, he looked almost charming.

During my last week, thoughts of college life, of what the future held were so sweet, getting into a smelly transit van at five in the morning didn't seem all that bad. I had done what needed to be done. I had my money saved. And although I was loath to admit it, I felt proud of myself. It was as if I'd been through some unedifying experience, and come out the other side all the stronger.

It rained for the majority of the week. Like a reward from above.

Late one morning, I was sweeping out the largest farm building. The doors banging open and shut didn't alarm me. A strong breeze had been doing that for the last hour. It was only when I felt a hand on my shoulder that I realized I wasn't alone.

Deano had sneaked in.

Grabbing my head, he forced his mouth over mine. I tried to push him away but he was far too strong. He threw me to the ground and jumped on top of me. With his knees across my chest, he pinned me down, trapping both my arms. Then he elbowed me in the nose. My eyes filled with water. All I could see were the outlines of things. A second blow knocked me out or senseless.

When I came to I could taste blood, and still feel the weight of his body and his rank smell all over me. Then his penis jabbed into my face, searching out my mouth. In frustration, he hit me again, pulled me over onto my front, wrenching my tracksuit bottoms down from the waist. I tried to seize up, to make it impossible, but he had his hand on the back of my neck, forcing my face into the dirt. When he ripped into me that initial pain turned everything off. It was as if I was watching it happen to somebody else.

Cold. Numb. I could hear the pitter-patter of rain, as Deano shunted himself up inside of me, grunting and moaning, twisting me this way and that.

When finished, he pushed his face against mine, licked my cheek and whispered, 'If you tell anybody about this, I'll fucking kill you.'

He stood up. His body cast a dark shadow over mine. And for some reason, having him staring down like that, when I was so broken and humiliated, felt more of a violation than what he'd just done to me. Too scared to move or look round, the next thing I heard was him zipping up his trousers. Then he spat on me and walked out.

THE END

Further titles by N A Randall

A Quiet Place to Die

MAD MARY

By Tony Wright

'You aren't listening to a word I'm saying are you?' Ivy crowed at her husband's cardigan-clad back.

Martin Benson pulled back a finger and the pristine net curtain floated back into place.

'What love?' he muttered, absently.

Ivy sighed. 'Never mind, what are you gawping at, anyway?'

'Mary's out again. She should be in a home or something.'

'Well you tried to arrange that and you know what happened.'

Martin shivered a little inside. He shambled over to his favourite armchair and plopped himself into it.

'She's harmless,' Ivy said crossing her flabby arms. 'This neighbourhood watch thing has driven you a bit cuckoo.'

'Harmless?' Martin scoffed, opening his newspaper. 'You've seen the state of her place. Bloody shithole, it is!'

'Language, Martin!' Ivy tutted sharply. 'If my mother were alive today—'

'She'd be a hundred and twenty!' Martin interrupted. He dropped his newspaper for a moment, a far-off frown creasing his face.

''S funny, thinking about it, Mary can't be younger than that. I've lived in this house all my life and I remember Mary being old when I was a nipper.'

'Don't be daft, man!' Ivy said, but, all the same, a strange feeling came over her.

After a moment, she shook it off briskly. 'Cup of tea, love?'

Stokely Road, as has been alluded to, was a Neighbourhood Watch area. And damned proud of it. Well, The Watch's organiser, Martin Benson was damned proud of it, anyway.

Indeed, the citizens of the whole street were, without fail, press-ganged into attending Martin's dreaded monthly meeting (you did get some tea and a slice of Ivy's renowned homemade Battenberg, though, so it wasn't all bad).

There could be no excuses for not turning up, except perhaps death. Some thought that even this reason might make Martin a bit cross though. He was that kind of man: officious, overbearing and opinionated with a grade A Napoleon complex thrown in. But he meant well, so people went along with it.

Stokely Road, itself, was a quiet estate that had been dropped unceremoniously in the middle of nowhere, sometime at the end of Queen Victoria's reign.

It had been built at the bottom of a slight hill. At the top of this crouched Stokely House, home of 'Mad Mary'.

It was a grim, forbidding edifice. Dark, gothic and blackened by the weather with a spacious, swampy garden that was overrun with weeds and enormous, unruly rose bushes that scratched ferociously at the few hardy souls who dared to walk up the cracked, mossy path.

The Addams Family might have thought twice about buying it as a home. Too much work to make it habitable, even for them.

Nearby Stokely Wood had long had a reputation as being a weird, even dangerous place.

Strange lights had been reported amongst the trees in the dead of night, local dogs would not enter after dusk and, stranger still, twenty years previously, the Right Rev. Ian Carmichael, vicar of All Saints Church in the nearest town, had disappeared whilst walking there one evening. He was never seen again.

Rumours of meetings in the woods by black magic cults and human sacrifice persisted and the finger was quietly pointed at the occupant of Stokely House from time to time.

Mary left the house rarely but, when she did, she was always seen in the same floppy hat (that may once have been blue…. it was difficult to tell with all the dirt on it) and long, all encompassing brown velvet coat.

She shuffled along slowly, staring at the ground, muttering darkly to herself.

The adults of Stokely Road, thought she was 'a bit funny', the kids thought she was a witch.

The local children often dared each other to scamper up the path of Stokely House and sing the song that all the locals knew:

"Mad Mary, Mad Mary, nothing in her head!
Mad Mary, Mad Mary, if she catches you you're dead!
Say your prayers, when up the stairs and quickly get to bed!
Or Mad Mary, Mad Mary will make you into bread!"

It was a rite of passage in the locality and you got extra bragging rights if you saw Mary staring furiously out of the window at you and didn't cry.

Occasionally a luckless (or too slow) child would be horrified to see the door, with its flaky black varnish and green stained brass knocker, flung open and find themselves face to face with the witch herself. They would get an earful of incomprehensible, banshee shrieking and flee in abject terror. That was something to tell your Grandchildren about.

Mary Stokely's story was often spoken about on the estate, but not truly known.

Mary, it was whispered, was the heiress to a long-ruined business empire who's father, driven insane by problems relating to a bad debt, had drunk and gambled his remain funds away in an orgy of wild, hedonistic parties and, well, orgies.

Some said she was distantly related to royalty, one of those in-bred throwbacks you hear about in the scandal sheets from time to time.

Perhaps she had been shunned by a true love, a tragic poet or struggling author (as they so often are) and had been driven mad with grief at her loss. For all anyone really knew, it could have been all of those.

Martin Benson's history with Mary went back to the day of his tenth birthday.

Martin had a gang, six in total, with him at the head.

Whilst out exploring the locale in that grubby, scuff-kneed way that gangs of kids used to in the days before XBoxes and IPhones, there was a challenge to Martin's leadership.

'Fatty' Pearson, the gang's self appointed second-in-command, who'd always fancied being in charge of the gang himself, loudly brought up the fact that Martin hadn't yet 'Run the Gauntlet'. This was a reference to the rite of passage at Stokely House and some of the other kids suddenly looked at Martin, their erstwhile leader, in a different light.

"E's right!' piped up 'Rubber' Johnny Davies amongst a chorus of mumbles and shuffling feet from the others.

Martin briefly considered punching 'Fatty's' stupid fat face in at this outrage, but the calm and cunning thinking that had got him where he was today, prevailed.

'Oh yeah, I forgot,' he said huffily.

So, the plan was formulated.

Later that day, Martin slinked, as slowly and quietly as he could, up Mary's path and readied himself to sing Mary's song whilst the others peeked out from behind the rambling hedge.

Suddenly, a pale ghastly face, topped with a grimy, blueish floppy hat appeared at the dirt streaked window.

Martin started and a small sharp yell escaped his fear dried lips. Without thinking, he picked up a stone from the path and threw it at the face, smashing a jagged hole in the window. Then he ran as if the devil himself (or *her*self, perhaps) was after him.

After that, Martin had felt that his card was marked, although nothing had never really happened after his adventure.

Even so, years later, he often felt like two shiny, white eyes were watching him from the dark windows of Stokely House.

This unease would never leave him and, when he grew up, he had petitioned the Council to have Mary put a home.

She was old, he would write. She needed looking after, he would inform the bored jobsworth at the other end of the telephone. Can't be good for her, all alone in that drafty, old house, he emailed to a whirring machine that promptly deleted this important missive.

Social Services *did*, eventually try their best.

Mary, for her part, cared not a jot for their attempts to introduce her to various places where other old folks waited for God in warm and pampered comfort.

She cared not for their efforts in getting her to at least get electricity installed in Stokely House (for it had none).

Any poor soul who dared to try to remove her from her home would soon retreat, followed down the path by dark, shrieking curses.

After a couple of years of this, Mary's file 'fell' down the back of a filing cabinet in the Town Hall basement and the everyone in officaldom promptly forgot who Mary Stokely was.

Martin's increasingly frantic attempts to reopen the case resulted in a visit from the Police and a caution for harassment of those 'hardworking public servants at the Council'.

Martin grudgingly had to admit defeat.

One fateful Halloween, the problem of what to do about Mary was solved.

The tradition of 'souling' existed for many years in Great Britain.

In days gone by, children would visit neighbouring homes and sing songs for the dead in exchange for cakes.

In latter times, this tradition has been loudly barged out of the way for its American mass-marketed equivalent, trick-or-treating.

Stokely Road's children were no less susceptible than their peers in the rest British Isles to such things and, in a carefully coordinated campaign admirable in its tenacity, relentlessly badgered their parents for permission to celebrate this ancient holiday. With gaudy fright masks, fake cobwebs that made your skin itch, plastic skeletons and all that good stuff.

Martin was rather sniffy about letting the rest of the Watch cart their offspring around the street begging for sweetmeats but, after many votes against him from tired out parents, a plan was agreed upon.

At 7pm on Halloween evening, a troupe of twelve miniature Witches, Zombies, Vampires, 'Skellingtons' and Princesses (not everybody liked monsters) started snaking their ragged way down Stokely Street. The line began at number 40. Jacinta and Harry, the yuppie couple living there, gave the puzzled kids some Bombay Mix, which they spat out and threw on the floor outside the gate.

I should mention here that the other part of this yearly tradition, tricking, had been expressly forbidden by Martin. No one would have rotten tomatoes flung at their doors if they'd forgotten to buy some fun sixed Mars bars for the little horrors on his watch. This was to be sternly enforced or everyone would be sent home without any sweets at all.

Two twins, going by the names of Simon and Stephen Greely, were not to be denied this pleasure, however, and secretly stashed a box of eggs about their person.

The twins were nine years old and had yet to 'Run the Gauntlet' at Mary's house.

Halloween was deemed the perfect day for them to rectify this.

As the other kids were herded, chattering and shrieking from door to door, the Greelys slipped away unnoticed.

At Mary's gate, they paused, took a deep breath and began the ritual, keeping their eyes glued to the window. Candle light flickered there but no sign of Mary was seen.

At the door, the Greely boys grasped their eggs in one hand and made ready to strike.

'Oi! What the bloody hell are you two up to?' Martin Benson's voice roared from the bottom of the path behind them. The boys swung around mouths agape. At that moment the front door was flung open and Mary stood there a dripping candle in her hand.

As she opened her mouth to shriek, the boys, in some strange echo of Martin's incident so long ago, let fly their eggs at the haggard figure.

Mary's mouth flapped shut in surprise as the eggs hit her full in the face and dropped her candle. There was an audible 'whoosh' as her long brown coat caught fire.

Hungry flames licked madly at the grimy material and Mary began to perform a macabre, but eerily graceful, pirouette as she burned.

Martin rushed forward and pulled the terrified boys away.

'Help her!' Stephen gasped.

Martin stared, temporarily frozen in fascination at Mary's hellish dance until the sound of running feet came up the path.

'Stay back!' Martin snapped. 'There's no helping her.'

This may or not have been true. Mary was now just visible as a screaming, ball of flame; more a hissing, crackling mannequin than a human.

Just before she collapsed into a smoking, sizzling heap, a blackened arm slowly reached out and pointed an accusing finger directly at Martin Benson.

No one blamed Martin for what had happened. Or the Greely boys either. It was a prank gone tragically wrong. It could have happened to anybody.

You might be thinking that Martin might even have been secretly relieved at Mary's demise. He wasn't though. He *was* a nosy, annoying busybody but he wasn't a bad man.

As it was, he took on a noticeably haunted, distant look that he never lost. Gone was the confident, pushy man everyone knew.

Mary had pointed at him before her death and he really seemed to have read something into that. Something that he would not talk about and not even Ivy, his wife of forty years, could coax out of him.

Martin wound up the Neighbourhood Watch soon after. His heart just wasn't in it anymore.

One year later, Ivy Benson came home from her weekly trip to the Bingo in nearby Stanton at 9 pm.

She knew instantly something was amiss. It was too quiet.

Normally, the TV would be blaring out some nonsense or other but Ivy could have heard a pin drop.

'What's that smell?' Ivy muttered to herself.

There *was* an odd smell in the hallway as she took her coat off. Not only that, but there was a hazy quality to the air. A thickness to the atmosphere that felt *wrong*.

'Martin?' Ivy said nervously as she approached the living room door. The metal door handle was warm to the touch.

She pushed open the door and walked in. A moment later she had crumpled to the floor in a dead faint.

Martin Benson sat unmoving in his favourite armchair. His cardigan and polyester slacks were fused to his blackened limbs.

His head was hairless and smoking. The skin cracked like crazy paving.

His wide eyes had popped in the heat and lazy wisps of smoke came from his silently screaming mouth.

A smudge of soot streaked the walls above the chair. In it, the baffled police later made out what looked very much like two letters, scrawled, perhaps, by someone's finger.

M.S.

THE END

Author's Note:

This story is, of course, fiction. However, when I was a very young lad, there really was a Mad Mary living just down the road from me. She wore a Floppy Blue hat, an ever present long brown coat (come rain or shine), lived in a flat (not a spooky mansion) without electricity and shouted incomprehensible things at everybody and everything that crossed her path. The theories whispered about the real lady's origins were very much as those I attribute to the fictional one.

The rest of it is probably made up.

Oh, and I don't know if Mary really was a witch or not.

Further titles by Tony Wright

The War of the Worlds: Aftermath
Holiday of the Dead

FREEDOM'S WINGS

By CW Lovatt

Freedom is infinity of choice.

I mention this because now Jennifer has decided to end things with me, *beaucoup* possibilities stretch out to the far distant horizon.

Way c-o-o-o-o-l!

She said, "It's not you, it's me."

"That sounds cliché," I tell her.

She replies, "You're right, it's not me, it's you."

"What?"

She said, "Well, for one thing, you're too argumentative."

"Me? *Argumentative?*"

"There you go again," she sighs.

"What?"

"Arguing."

"No I'm not."

"Yes you are."

"Fine, have it your way."

"It's not my way. It's just how it is."

"Fine."

"I hate when you do that."

"Do what?"

"When you say *'fine'* like that."

"I'm just agreeing." I point out – childishly, I suppose.

"That's bullshit and you know it." She doesn't seem geared for a fight. She sounds tired, but she keeps doggedly on. "You're being passive-aggressive. You'll never let anyone tell you anything."

"Whatever," I reply in my most agreeable tone, which, when you get right down to it, isn't all that agreeable.

But really, who can blame me? All this talk about leaving is getting me down. Worse than that, this is her apartment, so if anyone's going to leave, it's going to have to be me…and it's *raining* outside – one of those miserable cold, drizzling days that never seem to end. What kind of a person would kick someone out into something like that?

There was no denying this was the Mother of all Bummers, and must be dealt with accordingly.

"Okay, so I'm argumentative," I acknowledge the possibility while making a beeline to my stash. I don't know about you, but when I'm faced with the Mother of all Bummers, the only sure answer is the Mother of all Spliffs. "So okay, I can accept that maybe I might have to work on a few things. I'm cool with that – so unbelievably cool I don't think you understand how cool that *is*. I'm willing to work on myself. Like, I'm willing to expand my personality, to become a better person and all that stuff. So how cool is that?"

I think it is pretty cool.

"It's too late."

"Waddaya mean '*too late*'?" I ask, snipping a bud into tiny green flakes. I should probably be paying more attention to her, but a well constructed joint requires some serious attention in its own right. "I'm here. You're here. So let's talk. I mean, we can *talk*, can't we? We're two intelligent beings, aren't we? So how come we can't put our heads together and have a meeting of the minds? I mean, like, *c'mon* already!"

I cut up the bud and regard the little pile of shavings with a critical eye before deciding the Mother of all Spliffs requires further grandeur. I reach into the bag for another bud, and find there is only one left. This is indeed a bummer! I will have to give my guy a call. In the meantime, I recognize there are some serious issues needing resolution. I am okay with that. I mean, my mind is open and everything. I begin to cut up the second bud into tiny little snips.

Meanwhile, there is some hesitation at Jennifer's end - *serious* hesitation.

"I didn't want to get drawn into this," she said.

Man, she sounds tired.

"Drawn into what?" I ask, snipping carefully.

"Into *this*," she said with definite despair, "Into another argument! I just wanted to tell you we're through, that's all. I can't take another argument. It's all we do, and I just can't take it anymore."

Man, she's really in a bad place, all right. She sounds so forlorn I think of putting my arms around her, you know, to comfort her, but my hands are presently occupied.

"Hey, I don't want to argue, either," snip, snip. "Don't think it's *me* who wants to argue." Snip, snip, snip, "I just want for us to talk, I mean *really* talk. We can do that, can't we?"

"Well...."

"Sure we can. There isn't anything we can't solve if we work at it, is there? Relationships take work, don't they? I remember hearing that somewhere."

"I said that last night."

"Oh yeah? Well, that was good. I'll admit it. That *really* was a good one, babe, you know...*deep*. No spoken words were ever more true. You laid it down and I picked it up like....like it was *e.s.p.* or something. It just goes to show I'm tuned in, doesn't it?"

I scrape the clippings together and take out two papers – licking the glue on one before fastening it to the other. La Bomba, baby.

"You believe what you like," she said, ever so weary, "but the fact is you don't listen. You always want for us to talk, but you never listen."

"Sure I do." Rolling a double-paper spliff requires a great deal of concentration. Too much pressure and the seam will split. Not enough and you'll be left with something that looks baggy, and totally unprofessional. Maybe that sort of thing doesn't matter to some people, but it does to me. I mean, no question, you gotta take pride in your work.

"Have it your way," she shrugs, "it doesn't matter anymore."

Just a second. Just...one...more...second...almost there. I bring Gargantu-Joint to my mouth and lick the glued edge, smoothing it down. I regard the finished product with immense satisfaction. Few things are so rewarding.

"Aw c'mon, babe. Don't say that. It *has* to matter. I mean, look at all the time we've spent together. Doesn't that count for anything?"

"You only moved in two weeks ago."

"Whoa! *Really*?" I light the joint, inhaling deeply, being careful to keep air flowing on the outside as well as inside to make the coal burn brighter. I suck the smoke down into my lungs and keep it there. Then I hold the reefer out for her.

She hesitates, regarding my creation almost as though she doesn't trust it. My thoughts are that this is very strange. There are few things in this world I trust more than the weed. The weed is my friend. He will never let me down. He will always listen with respect. He will never bust my balls when things get weird.

In the end, she accepts it. She takes a short, girly drag and hands it back. It is a ceremony, like smoking a peace pipe.

I let the smoke out of my lungs. It billows and clouds between us. I hack and cough and cough and hack. My guy sells me some really primo shit. He is a good guy. In fact, he is one of the most truly superlative guys on the face of the planet.

"So, two weeks," I manage before I am spluttering and coughing again. "I mean, I guess I realized that, it's just we seemed to...you know...fit so well it seems longer."

41

I take another long and lovely pull on Mr. Super-Spliff. I must have been tense, because already I can feel myself relaxing. It is no good feeling overly stressed in this day and age. I have heard somewhere that heart disease is the number one killer in the nation.

"You had nowhere else to go," she said, once more accepting the joint, "so I took you in. I felt sorry for you."

I kind of remember that. Tracey had just kicked me out. That had been after two whole months together – which was something of a record. I mean, we could have been in *love*, or something. That almost made it *tragic*, didn't it?

"You were all alone, like a lost puppy, so I took you in."

"Hey yeah, thanks." I am beginning to feel very fine. There is too much reality in the world. I, for one, will have none of it. "That was really good of you – really *humane*. You could have left me standing out in the rain, but you took me in. I owe you, *big* time."

"I felt sorry for you," she repeated, "you know, after what happened to your brother and all. Even though it's been over a year, you seem to be having trouble dealing with it. I thought I could help, but I was wrong."

Fu-u-u-u-u-ck! Low blow or *what*! Why'd she have to suddenly go and bring Eddie into all this?

I suck in another massive toke. Getting over this bummer is going to require some very real dedication on my part. Throwing my brother's memory in my face – you know, just out of the blue like that - was serious shit indeed! I mean, what was *that* all about?

I continue toking on the spliff. There is nothing I feel like saying so I just keep on pulling, watching with an appreciative eye while the coal burns brighter and brighter.

I guess she caught my vibe because after a while she said, "I'm sorry, I shouldn't have mentioned that."

Man, that coal was bright. Already it has burned down half the length of the joint, which is really something when you consider how moist I keep the weed. It's probably not a good idea to be wasting it like this, but I can't seem to be able to bring myself to stop. I just keep pulling and pulling until I'm full of the smoke, like…like I'm a hot air *balloon*, or something!

Then I think, 'Hey, wouldn't that be far out – to be a hot air balloon?'

And suddenly, like a miracle, it happens; I *am* a balloon, bobbing gently in the warm summer air. I am one of dozens of brilliant colours on a huge green field of blossoming ganja. All of us are tugging on ropes binding us to the earth, each of us eager to take to the friendly skies. I can feel the sun on my face, and feel the heat inside that insists on propelling me upward. We all want to break free; to escape. Who *wouldn't* want that? I trust that heat like I trust the weed. We are one...we are brothers.

Then, for one last time, I'm back in her apartment.

"Know what?" I said, "You're right. We gave it our best shot, but I can see it's a no-go. I'll just get my stuff and leave, okay? No hard feelings?"

"I'm sorry," she repeats, but she is right. It is too late.

I go through her drawers, shoving my stuff into two garbage bags. I'm not sure, but maybe in my haste, I shove a pair of her panties in there as well. The bags are the same ones I'd used when moving in, can you believe that? There must have been some sort of inner voice at work when I'd unpacked to make me toss them in the closet instead of throwing them out like a normal person.

I accept the gift of a third bag to pull over my guitar – it's still raining – and I'm ready. I've become something of a legend over how quickly I can be gone from a former place of residence.

Eyes brimming, she waits for me at the door.

"I wish..." her voice trembles. Apparently, she is expecting one of those teary goodbyes.

"It's okay," I put the bags down and give her a feather-light embrace. "Everything'll turn out so amazingly alright you won't even believe it, just wait and see."

She starts to snuffle. That's my cue. I pick up my stuff and leave.

Freedom is infinity of choice.

As I set off down the street, misty rain plastering hair to skull, my mind is a split screen. One half is brooding on the day when Eddie chose Crystal Meth over me. The other is a severing of bonds over green fields, and a cascade of every colour in the rainbow rushing joyfully toward the sun – toward heaven itself, if we can get there.

My brother was free – none freer.

I hope that, somewhere out there, he still is.

THE END

Further titles by CW Lovatt

The Adventures of Charlie Smithers

IN NOMINE PATRIS
SINE SPIRITU, SINE FILIO, DAMNARI IN AETERNUM

By Poppet

*(In the name of the **father**,*
without the son, without the holy spirit, forever damned)

Chapter 1: Conversionis Pagani
(The Conversion of the Heathen)

This is not what I expected. How can they cram us into these dungeons when the monks have such luxury? When the church of Saint Paul is bedecked in finery a queen would envy?

"Laura!" screeches the banshee in a wimple and habit, "I said kneel!"

Panicked, I move to comply, elbowing for room, the gravel skinning my kneecaps when the dyke in black shoves me to the ground with a hard strike of her elbow between my shoulder blades.

"Jesus!" I snap.

The bitch clearly went to gladiator school before joining the holy ranks.

Wet leather connecting with my face registers after the agony, "We do not use the lord's name in vain! Blasphemy will be whipped out of you."

Where's the love? Where is Jesus? Why are they so savage?

"I was calling for his mercy, sister," I snap back, regretting it the second the high pressure hose blasts me to the point of drowning.

It's agonizing, bruising eyeballs, filling my mouth and nasal cavity, forcing me to inhale frigid fluid until I'm puking it back up, suffocating. Powerless, I'm pinned to the raw brick wall by the unholy water-pressure, holding me prisoner in the baptism of fury.

Prone and prostrate, desperate to catch air, the grip on my head barely registers until warm scalp freshly razored comes into contact with the next canon of cold.

Fuck you all!

"Bitch!" I struggle, crawling until the bricked corner severs my escape and I'm unceremoniously scalped for my sins.

*

A month in a cell the size of a broom closet, I can now relate to poor little Harry Potter. I've been stripped of my identity and renamed Mary. Do I look like a Mary to you? Fuck no!

I'm clothed in burrel and it scratches and chafes worse than chickenpox. My scalp is still scabbed and my body is a battleground of carnage.

Various shades of purple and greened-yellow mottle flesh in the blessings of bruises for my smart mouth and desire to defy the dictators. How is the garb worn by the nuns any different to a burqa? What fucking century are we in?!

I'd rather be a Cluniac monk, they at least get to wear black.

My underwear looks like I joined the Mormon church of the 1620's. If they don't supply tampons I swear I will curse my mother into her afterlife, damning her soul for an eternity for doing this to me. Not to mention there is no contraception in the holy see. *If* I escape, or one of those randy fuckers gets out of hand, I will be royally fucked.

Self pity envelops me and I stare at my hands still pink from scrubbing the monk's toilets. No toilet brushes, oh no. Hand deep in shit is the way it works around here.

Tears are adored, I refuse to cry. *I won't.* I will never give them the satisfaction.

How is the church any different to the Klu Klux Klan? Their symbol was a cross too, a sigil doesn't make you holy. Actions speak louder than words, hypocrites! The ridiculous garments don't make you devout. And the fanaticism is identical, the only difference is these assholes call it spiritual cleansing instead of ethnic cleansing.

Kneeling on the burlap mat which comprises my bed, I look out at the perfect day barely visible through the thick iron mesh in the tiny square serving as air and lighting.

You'd swear I was abducted into the dark ages in the middle of the Inquisition, not sent for reform by parents who think alcohol is the devil's juice. I called them hypocrites because they serve wine in church.

Dominatrix Superior yanked my studs after the naked scrubbing of our sins, severing piercings by tearing them out without undoing them. My body was ruddy and livid for a week after being wire brushed raw, our initiate blood flooding over the concrete of the inner sanctum while the

45

perverted bastards stood on the upper level watching the breasts and vaginas of teenage girls the way pedophiles lust after buggering.

Shifting because my muscles keep seizing, I dare to relax. It's insane to expect anyone to spend fourteen hours on their knees without moving. I can't believe this shit is legal. I now understand why parents may not visit their offspring for six months. It'll take that long to heal the damage visible to the naked eye.

It'll take that long to break us.

Where is the salvation in shaving off our hair? It's an old testament commandment from Leviticus. Shaving off the hair atones, and it shames. Medieval doesn't come close to describing the savage abuse in god's temple.

Now I'm a skinhead punk hidden in a habit. As Christ suffered for our sins, we must suffer for ours. The liturgy of penance, which if we don't adhere to shall subject us to flagellation as Christ was flogged by the Romans before crucifixion. '*Suffer little children*', Matthew 19 vs 14.

I can't believe how they've brainwashed their shitty indoctrination into me.

And suffer we do. Suffer we will. Long live the god of suffering and humiliation.

Call it what you will, this is a cult of sadists.

There is no god of love inside these walls.

My guardian angel walked away when I was forced under duress to marry Jesus Christ and accept him as my lord and savior.

They mock me by calling me Mary. Mary would cry to see how they've perverted her son Immanuel into a Roman construct of fear and misery.

For fuck's sake, if they just stopped to examine their tomes with any logic they'd be forced to concede that the dudes writing about walking on water and raising the dead were smoking some seriously good shit. The shrooms in the stew were a bit funky. It was the crystal meth of the forefathers who wrote down their hallucinations which are now gospel.

"Mary!"

Shocked out of my reverie I snap to face the angel of death, her spiteful face the epitome of our blessed father in heaven who does not offer love or 'rest', but misery for comfort and pain for salvation.

"You are not praying. Child I have no choice, you will be sent to Father Déyment. How do you expect God to forgive you if you do not repent?"

"Fuck your god," I spit in her face when she lynches me in her biting grip, but my body betrays me.

I am quaking in fear, knowing too well the pain waiting to visit my accosted body in a fresh assault of debased humiliation.

Chapter 2: Sancti Crypta, Nostri Superni Diabolus
(The Holy crypt of our heavenly devil)

I have spent more years than I know in service to the gods of misery. Shipped off to a mountain shrine before the allotted visiting day arrived, I have sacrificed hope in exchange for despair.

There is no escape for those of us sentenced to this incarceration surrounded with rock.

I watch each new March with utter terror. Juvenile delinquents no older then ten are cast off to the care of the everlasting love and forgiveness of Cardinal Déyment.

Oh yes, he sure moved up in the world, getting to wear his favorite color, the color of sacrifice and blood.

I dare to assume we are in the isolated region of the Pyrenees. The irony isn't lost on me, but I play my part, pretending to worship while clutching the little black book of Satanic creed.

For Satanic it is.

I have read it, cover to cover, many many times, and still this ossuary with its crypts and bones curdles my blood. How they can call tombs holy, worshipping mummies, it is beyond my ability to comprehend. If I question I am punished, and I've had a life supply of the bitter panacea at the hands of the holy dis-order.

Walking quickly to the accommodations of the new initiates, the screaming halts my steps. Dropping to my knees in the rectory I clutch my rosary, begging for the abuse to end.

"Please, if there is a god, save us from your followers, their zealous inhumanity is slicing my soul. Save me, save them, please," I beg, tears blossoming across my retinas.

Bastards! Fucking bastards!

No angel alights, no celestial harpers raise the roof, no rapture to snatch us from their wicked claws.... was it all just a book of lies?

I will not stand by while that sick prick baptizes his dick in underage blood.

No one can hear their screams but the co-conspirators, and the deaf and blind sisters I have for company.

47

They're old and senile and too far gone to care.

Oh yes, god delivers so many blessings on those in his secluded care.

Rage thunders down my spine, hardening my muscles and my resolve. I grab the hefty mass copy of the bible, testing its weight in my hand while rushing silently down the corridor.

No more children will suffer to enter the kingdom of heaven. Not on my fucking watch!

Bursting into his chambers where he has his thick erection hilt deep in Jonathan Smith's rectum I slam the book against his skull, whacking him back so as to deliver as little pain to the latest victim as possible.

Déyment rounds on me, lunacy ripe in his eyes, high on the demonic ambrosia of tearing flesh to slake his defiling libido. "Mary!"

"Not Mary you cunt! My name is Laura!" Smashing his face with the spine of god's unholy gospels, I shove him with my shoulder, ramming him into the bookshelf, yelling at the broken child, "Run! Run for your life, and scream the world down! This is his shame, not yours!"

Déyment is not a halfling, he's not weak, he's a bear of a bastard who rounds on me to punch me flat in the face, so hard the world charcoals instantly.

The smell of semen and blood ferments my nostrils, reminding me vividly of how nuns stay 'virgins' while surrounded by psychopaths who fuck each other when they think no one is watching.

The degradation I suffered will scar my soul long after my demise. I lift my arm defensively, warding off blows, spitting through the blood in my mouth, "Immanuel was the last sacrifice. No more shall blood be spilt for the god Molech. He said, **I am making a new covenant**."

Blood trickles down my ear, blocking it in a hot tickle, but I continue holding up the book as my witness to accuse the devil of treachery, "People of Israel! It was not to me that you slaughtered and sacrificed animals for forty years in the desert. It was the tent of the god Molech that you carried, and the image of Rephan, your star god; they were idols that you made to worship! **Acts eight verse forty-two!**" I scream at him. "Molech is a false god, the god of sacrifice and fire! God is love! There is no sacrifice for god! You are an evil devil blasphemously calling yourself holy!"

Crawling away, my bones numbing from the assault, vertigo steals my stability. I am hysterical when I screech, "**My children, keep yourself from false gods! One John five verse twenty-one!**"

He's pawing at my face, vicing it between his knees, muffling my curses of truth, "The beast was given authority over every tribe, nation, language, and race. All people living on earth worship it! Revelation fourteen! Who is the beast, Father? He's a satan **who deceived the whole world!** Revelation twelve verse nine!"

"**You are the children of your father the devil**, and you want to follow your father's desires. From the very beginning he was a **murderer** and has never been on the side of truth, because **there is no truth in him**... He who comes from God listens to God's words. **You, however, are not from god**, and that is why you will never listen. John 8 vs 44-47."

The blade is so sharp I don't realize what he's doing until he's done it. My mouth rapidly fills with blood, burning my throat with the vile stain of coppery haemoglobin.

"My god, Déyment! What have you done!?" bellows Father Walsch, rushing into the sanctum of chaos.

In shock, unable to breathe, crying with realization why Mother Deborah is deaf, and why Sister Ruth is blind.

He has made me a mute! He has cut out my tongue! He's holding it in his hand as flaccid as his still exposed and bloodied penis!

Vomiting uncontrollably, his response is dull in the dizzy rush of panic in my ears, "Sister Mary has taken the vow of silence."

It's too little epiphany too late. Women and children are the targets. I read it just this morning.

The dragon was furious with the woman and went off to fight against the rest of her descendants, Revelation 13. All children come from women, we do not suffer to enter the kingdom, we suffer for vengeance.

Bleeding out, gagging through the gurgles, my accusations and proof using their own book have been silenced.

Triumphant I stare up at the leaking dick between the akimbo legs blocking my view of the ceiling. I have witnessed, now I die for my courage, but you forget Cardinal Déyment, you forget John twenty. *If you forgive people's sins, they are forgiven. If you do not forgive them, they are not forgiven.*

We will never forgive you.

I will never forgive you.

Never.

THE END

49

Further titles by Poppet

Darkroom Saga Books
Satanarium (Darkroom Saga Book 2)
Over Exposure (Darkroom Saga Book 3)
Wrapture (Darkroom Saga Book 4)
Quislings
Dusan
Penance

THE RAT-CATCHER

By Scott Stanford

I open the front door as a small burst of horror perspires along my forehead, final notices and unpaid bills greeting me after another nightshift. I'm so tired that the panic quickly dies, depression anchoring me down as I kick them under the carpet and make my way upstairs.

I had to leave Jenny alone again last night, it's the third time this week and I hate it, hate the thought of her being alone if some crackhead decides to rob us, but I can't afford a babysitter. She knows better than to let anyone in, especially since the last time, but that's not all that bothers me, it's leaving her alone with the rats. I found a nest of them in the basement yesterday and a couple managed to get upstairs before I noticed. I took care of the ones I could catch in the most humane way I could think of, and then spent hours trying to find the other two, but no luck. My neighbour told me the rat problem in this area goes hand in hand with the druggies, and that didn't make me feel any better.

I've only been in the house for five minutes and I have to rub my hands together for warmth, we had our central heating cut off two days ago and at this time of year I think it's warmer outside than it is in here. At least we have a roof over our heads I suppose, that's what I tell myself as I knock on Jenny's bedroom door, but as I open it everything changes. Speechless at first I look in to see her lying asleep, breathing heavily as a big black rat sits on her stomach. Almost as if it's watching her, squinting its beady eyes and twitching its diseased mouth I panic, grabbing one of Jenny's magazines and rolling it quickly. As fast as I can, hoping to catch it unaware I leap at the animal, hitting it with enough force to knock it from the bed. Watching it fall to the floor, staring in hope that its dead Jenny wakes with a surprised, *'What's happening?'* as I quickly turn to her, ushering her out of bed with, *'Get ready for school, you'll be late,'* making sure she doesn't see the dead rat.

On my hands and knees I scrub the floor, the dead rat in a carrier bag besides me as I clean away its faeces and throw the dirty rag in on top of it. I feel sick having to do it, sick and tired, so much so that I slump on the floor and don't want to get up, closing my eyes to see bills from the mortgage lender and hearing rats scurrying through my skull. Though all it takes is, *'Daaad!'* to bring me back, echoing through the cold house as Jenny shouts, *'It's going cold!'*

Making my way downstairs I see a cup of tea on the table and a few pieces of burnt toast on the plate in front of me. *'What's this?'* I smile as she sits opposite, replying, *'Just being nice, sorry it's not buttered,'* as I grin, *'That's fine, who needs butter,'* trying to act as believable as possible as I catch sight of the black tea. *'Or milk,'* I add, giving a deep sigh with, *'I'm sorry, I'll pick some up later,'* feeling like dirt as I start to sink, staring blankly at the table as she reaches for my hand. Ashamed I raise my head, looking at her as she chirps, *'It helps if you dip the toast in the tea,'* without a care. *'You're right,'* I say, forcing a smile as she replies, *'Well I am getting older,'* with a cocky tilt of her head. Striking me as an odd thing to say I ask, *'What do you...'* but as I notice the joy in her eyes slightly fade I remember it's her birthday on Thursday. *'You didn't forget did you?'* she asks with a crushed expression, so I lie, *'Of course not,'* with a wide smile on my face, letting it mask as I imagine the money leaking from my overdrawn account. *'So you're buttering me up huh?'* I deflect, unintentionally causing her to laugh, *'Good one dad,'* as she waves a piece of dry toast in the air. *'So what do you want for your birthday?'* I ask trying to hide a pained expression, seeing her scrunch her face in thought as she beams, *'A pony!'* Drinking my black tea I almost spit it out with, *'Sweetie, we haven't got room for a pony,'* and without missing a beat she replies, *'You're right, how about a cat?'* Jumping from her seat and not expecting an answer she kisses me on the cheek with, *'I'm gonna miss the bus,'* as she runs out of the kitchen. Leaving me dumbfounded I shout, *'Have a nice day,'* as the door closes behind her, looking to the burnt toast on my plate with an attempted smile.

Making my way to bed I hear a noise coming from the basement, a scratching sound that niggles in my ear. Exhausted and almost certain at what I'll find I open the door and turn on the light, looking down the stairs as I see a horde of rats carpeting the ground, scurrying along as they hiss. Slamming the door shut I shake my head, unable to handle it right now, too tired to do anything but sleep.

Four hours, that's how long I slept before driving back to work, clocking in and finding myself back at the manufacturing line as Michael tells me about his niece Tabatha. She went missing three weeks ago and no one knows where to, the police can't find a trace and the parents are in a state. The more he talks about it the more it bothers me, makes me think of Jenny going home to an empty house, alone till I get home at nine. After a while I change the topic, tell him about the rat problem, that pest control want two hundred pounds to get rid of them, giving me no choice but to take care of it myself. So he tells me about his brother's friend, someone who used to work for 'Killpest' who does a little bit of business on the side, cheaply. Intrigued I ask for his number, writing it on the back of my hand with, *'And what's him name?'* *'I don't know, he's just a damn rat-catcher,'* Michael says, sneakily sipping from a hipflask asking, *'So what you getting Jenny for her birthday?'* *'At this rate a rat-catcher, but I need to get her something nice, she never asks for anything y'know, not even sweets,'* I grump, letting him spiel, *'You know what my dad got me for my eight birthday? One of those transforming robots.'* *'That's not so bad,'* I say, half focusing on work and watching him take another swig as he laughs, *'Next day the police came around, my old man stole it from the neighbour's kid.'*

It's twenty-past nine before I get home, Jenny's birthday present in the trunk and twenty minutes later than I expected. Pulling up outside the house I see a white van parked across the street, waving my hand at who I think is the rat-catcher as he nods back at me. Running across the road the first thing I do is apologise, hearing a muffled, *'Not to worry'* as he pulls at the red scarf wrapped around the lower half of his face. *'Do you want to take a look inside?'* I ask, watching him move to the back of his van as he replies, *'That won't be necessary, if it's rats you got we'll have them sorted for you in a few days.'* Watching him open the van he taps his hand on a large cage, running it along the plastic cover concealing what's inside as he says, *'Best way to get rid of vermin is naturally, I've got a starving possum in here and she'll do all the work for you.'* *'I didn't think we had possum's in Britain,'* I say curiously, causing him to slightly whisper, *'We don't, that's why this is…off the books.'* Moving from the cage and placing a hand on the door he asks, *'but if you're uncomfortable with it…'* causing me to reply *'No, no, no,'* as he seems wary. *'It's not a problem but, how much?'* I ask, relieved to hear, *'Thirty quid,'* as I snap up the offer with, *'Sounds great.'* Reaching back to the cage he remarks, *'She's a big one,'* lifting it from the van as he warns, *'Possum's are nocturnal so keep her covered at all times and in the dark. Put her where the rats are and she'll eat them all, open her cage at night then close it again in the morning. That's it really, but don't get too close, she don't care too much for humans. I'll pick her up in two days and you can pay me then, all good?'* Quickly replying, *'All good,'* the only thing I can think of is the money I've saved, feeling a little better about spoiling Jenny for her birthday.

Watching the rat-catcher drive away I walk to the house but leave the possum and Jenny's presents outside, making sure the coast's clear first. Looking at my watch and thinking she's probably in bed I get startled as a loud sound comes from the kitchen, moving quickly with my fists clenched as I look in with surprise. Seeing Jenny stand on the counter as she looks on top of the cupboards I ask, *What are you doing?*' watching her jump down with a coy, *Nothing.*' Without a word, just giving her a stern glare she admits, *Looking for presents, it's my birthday tomorrow,*' and adding, *Look what Shelley made for me,*' as she holds out her hand to show a brightly coloured bracelet made of beads, each painted to spell her name. With an innocent expression on her face, doughy eyes and her hands folded in front of her I ask, *You think you're cute don't you?*' Pinching a forefinger and thumb together she smiles, *A little,*' and I can't help but return the expression, kissing her on the forehead with, *Get to bed, I'll be up to tuck you in in a minute.*'

Standing in the hallway I watch Jenny run upstairs, hearing her bedroom door close before I step outside and grab her presents first. Placing them on the counter, on top of the bills and unopened warnings two large stuffed animals stare at me, a cat and a pony as I look into their plastic eyes mouthing, *I hope she likes you.*' Next comes the cage, and with it I quickly make my way to the basement, the weight heavier than I expected. Opening the door and reaching for the light I quickly change my mind, childishly grunting, *Nocturnal, duh!*' as I make my way down the stairs. Hearing the rats crawl around my feet, their hisses and scratching causing me to bite, *Wait and see what I got for you,*' I place the cage down and open it swiftly. Surprised that the possum moves so quickly I barely see the outline of its body, darting into the shadows as I hear the rats squeal, a massacre unfolding.

After sitting on the couch for an hour, wrapping Jenny's presents and hiding them in the kitchen I make my way to bed, stopping by the basement door and opening it to shine down a torch light. Curious of what a possum looks like I catch a glimpse of its long body, running into hiding as I see the half eaten remains of rats spread along the ground. Closing the door, hoping that it finishes the rest before morning I try to shake the image, wondering if there's enough eggs in the kitchen to make Jenny pancakes for breakfast.

Fast asleep I suddenly find myself jumping from the bed as a loud sound echoes through the house. At first thinking it's someone trying to break in I run to Jenny's room, seeing her bed empty and calling, *Jenny!*' as loud as I can. A guilty *Yeah?*' comes from downstairs and I feel relieved at the sound of her voice, confident she's looking for presents as she joyfully shouts, *Daddy you got me a cat!*' Smiling to myself and preparing to make an early breakfast a sudden scream drowns me in fright, so I run downstairs, seeing the basement door open. *No, no, no*' I mutter to myself, moving as fast as I can and turning on the light, losing my footing in panic and tumbling down the stairs.

Winded at first I cough, opening my eyes to see Jenny's body lying unconscious on the floor. Unscathed and slowly coming around I tap her cheek to see her eyes open, smiling at her as a hissing sound comes from the shadows. Slowly changing to a growl I watch in horror as the animal emerges, its claws scratching at the floor and furred body hunched, walking almost like a human. I stare at its long snarling snout, its mouth filled with human teeth and tearing eyes a bright pitiful blue. Screeching, *'Help me!'* its voice resembling a young girl's I notice something on its wrist, a bright coloured bracelet made of beads, each painted to spell her name, Tabatha. Clutching Jenny close to me, unsure of what to do I hear, *'Jenny will like working for me!'* come from the top of the stairs, looking up to see the rat catcher as he slowly unravels his red scarf, causing my lips to tremble in horror, begging, *'Please, not my daughter!'*

THE END

Further titles by Scott Stanford

Dorothy (The Darker Side of Oz Book 1)
Abaddon Rising (The Darker Side of Oz Book 2)

SCATO - ILLOGICAL

By A J Kirby

Daniel scanned the office, eyes narrowed to slits. He sniffed at the ripe air, nostrils flapping away like he was trying to determine the source of the smell. Like he didn't know; like he couldn't see the goddamned public toilet that the room had become. Gave his verdict: 'Hate to say I told you so, but I did warn you something like this might happen.'

I had to stifle my desire to choke the life out of him right then and there, in front of Jackie and *that thing*. Way he said it, with such relish dripping off his thick, slippery tongue, you could tell he loved every goddamned 'I told you so' minute.

Maybe that's what all psychiatrists are like. Maybe they all just sit back, wait for merry hell to break loose and then get that self-satisfied, *if you'd listened to me in the first place, everything would have been tickety-boo* gleam in their eyes.

When I bought Jackie the doll, Daniel was full of snide comments. Over breakfast, he told me that I was stupid, reinforcing gender stereotypes like that. Over lunch, he said I should have bought her a model aircraft, or some other boy's toy. Over supper, he told me that I'd end up giving my own daughter some kind of disorder.

But I *think* I bought *that thing* to spite him. Think I bought it just so Daniel would be able to spout all of his usual claptrap and then maybe, just maybe, I'd get so angry I'd finally get the nerve to boot him into touch.

Jackie, of course, was delighted with her new toy. She's a sweet girl: when you give her a present, she reacts just like your perfect daughter would. As though she'd never expected that she'd be presented with anything but crap.

Soon as she saw the doll, she gushed. 'Thankoo! This is the bestest present I could wish for.'

'Don't use the word get,' muttered Daniel. 'It's a weak little word. Try *receive* instead.'

Jackie nodded politely, but clearly wasn't listening. She was fascinated by the doll: its paisley-print dress just like hers, and the soft hair which felt so real… She stopped pushing that pram of hers around, put the brakes on her constant colouring and gave up juggling.

The thing I came to realise was that the doll took a fair bit of looking after. It was much more advanced than the ones they had in my youth. This one, for example, regularly shat herself. As it turned out, the doll was a regular little shit machine. Despite the fact that she didn't – couldn't – eat, she still managed to manufacture whole sewage plants of the stuff. And so, little Jackie had to grow up fast. She had to learn all about nappies and bum creams.

The first time the doll shat itself, Jackie was delighted. Called me up to her room to have a look. 'Isn't it great,' she enthused. 'Look at all that poop. I'm so proud.'

Unaccountably, Jackie named the doll Daniel, despite it quite obviously being a girl. I found this quite fitting, after what the real Daniel had said about gender stereotypes.

She became inseparable from the thing. She would wander through the house muttering to it. I mean, she'd always talked a lot - she kept up this constant monologue of seemingly nonsensical chatter - but with the doll, it began to get quite unnerving. It was as though they were in their own private little world that we were excluded from.

After a while, Daniel took me aside for one of his little talks. 'There's something not quite right about that doll,' he said. 'Look at those eyes. They seem like they're following you.'

He was right. The eyes weren't the usual taxidermist's buttons: they were little fiery things which seemed to sparkle with knowledge. But I didn't let on to Daniel that I agreed with him. I just let things go…

And now look at the mess we're in.

Mess would be a euphemism actually.

Suppose I should have heeded the warnings. The not-too-happy coincidence that in the very first week Jackie unwrapped that doll, the sewer system under our street suddenly became blocked. Men from the council were sent down to look at the pipes. Came back up chocolate-coated but shaking their heads, darned if they could figure out what the problem might be.

All our neighbours were flocked on their lawns, muttering and moaning. I heard that at the Willis house on the corner the toilet had literally exploded, with old man Willis right there on the throne. I couldn't help but laugh. Old man Willis was an ornery old crone. Once upon a time I'd had very strong suspicions that he might have poisoned Jackie's rabbit when it escaped and crapped in his garden. Suppose Willis got his crappy comeuppance.

Jackie, who was standing close to us, but kinda withdrawn too, turned round to look at me. She was clutching the Daniel-doll close to her chest. From where I stood, it looked as though the doll was whispering in her ear.

But that's a stupid idea, isn't it?

'Shit happens,' Jackie said. She fixed us all with fiery eyes and then smiled. She'd never sworn before. Never even said 'damn' and yet here she was putting into crude language exactly what each one of the neighbours were thinking.

Of course, I had to pretend to punish her. Daniel especially wanted me to come down hard on her. 'She has to learn boundaries,' he told me. 'Godda learn there's is a difference between what you can *think* about saying, and what you actually say.'

Daniel was sitting in his makeshift office – in reality our single-door garage. He was making a cat's cradle of his long fingers, the way that men like him do when they are governing other people's lives.

'But she's only a little girl.'

Daniel swung round on his office chair and flicked through a stack of important papers on his desk. For a moment, I thought I'd been summarily dismissed, but then he pulled out a photocopied page.

'That's from the Dictionary of Psychology,' he said. He pointed to the definition of something called 'scatology'. 'Read it.'

Scatology, it turned out, was a preoccupation with lewdness and filth, as symbolised by shit. As I finished reading, Daniel raised his eyebrow.

'You don't want your little girl growing up like that do you? Get rid of the doll that shits itself.'

Meekly, I nodded.

Still I didn't make Jackie lose the doll. Oh, there were plenty of opportunities. Like when she was asleep with the doll in her bed. The heady scent of shit underscoring the usual talcum smell of her room. But I couldn't bring myself to do it.

For some reason, it felt as though the doll was about the only thing that Daniel didn't have control over in our house.

When I realised that things were getting serious it was too late.

Daniel and I had been out the back enjoying the sun, trying to ignore the lingering stink from the blocked pipes. For a few weeks now, the neighbourhood had all been forced to queue up outside hastily erected portaloos while the councilmen tried to discern the problem. In those weeks, I'd found out rather more about my neighbours than I felt it necessary to know. Mrs. Bickerstaffe, for example left brontosaurean skid-marks on the pan. Miss Carson only liked to use the john when she thought everyone else was asleep: I'd see her sneaking out in her pink slippers and dressing gown at all sorts of strange hours.

Anyway, we were out back. Daniel reading, me staring through the fence at the portaloos trying to see whether old man Willis would ever deign to use them. Surely he couldn't have corked it for that long... I was absently considering this when, inexplicably, I got this creeping feeling at the back of my neck. I had this sudden thought – like a physical stabbing sensation really –I hadn't seen Jackie for a long time. She usually floats about, interfering and sticking her nose in. It was so rare that we got a moment's quiet that I'd become less vigilant than I should have been.

So anyway, I jumped up. Rushed back into the house. Found her almost immediately, all curled up on the sofa, tears in her eyes. Took me a while to notice that there was this awful smell clogging the atmosphere of the room. This smell was far worse than the stink in the streets or the night-time shit-scent from the doll's nappy.

It was like something had crawled into the room and died a violent death.

'What's that smell?' I asked, moving over to stroke her hair.

She jumped at my touch.

'I'm sorry, mommy,' she blubbered. 'It wasn't me.'

It was only when I perched on the edge of the sofa next to her I took in what had happened to the television.

'What the hell've you done?' I asked, trying to keep a tight leash on my mad-dog anger. 'Are you going to tell me, Little Miss, how shi... sorry, poop, came to be smeared all over the screen?'

'Daniel telt me that he didn't want me to watch. Said if I watched, then he'd get mad.'

'Don't be ridiculous,' I seethed. 'Daniel's a doll. Daniel can't tell you to do anything. Where is that damned thing?'

'On my bed, mommy.'

And that's when I screamed for the real Daniel to get his ass back in the house. Of course, we all trooped up to Jackie's room, Daniel muttering all sorts of threatening crap about gender stereotypes coming back to haunt me.

But right then, I didn't care.

I just wanted my little girl to be all right.

The Daniel doll wasn't in the room, but that clinging shit-stink was.

'The hell's that coming from?' groaned Daniel.

'That's right, Daniel.' There was a tiny smile playing on Jackie's lips. 'That's the smella hell.'

All thoughts of punishing her for using the 'h' word were soon put out of our minds when we heard the huge wheezing, cracking, breaking sound coming from the bowels of the house. It sounded like a bubbling, growling sound that your stomach makes after a hearty meal, only magnified or put through mega Marshall amps strapped to loudspeakers.

And suddenly we all knew where both the smell and the sound were coming from. They were bellowing up from Daniel's cosy office in the garage.

We all descended the stairs. Into hell, I couldn't help but think.

Daniel fumbled with the keys, didn't see the lumpy brown liquid that was seeping out from under the door. Finally, he opened it.

How we all came to be standing in the office. The cute doll was tucked up on the desk, surrounded by Daniel's precious papers. She wasn't moving, wasn't grinning, wasn't laughing. But part of me kind of expected her to be...

Because in all my life, I have never seen such a huge amount of shit. It was dripping from the light-shade, had darkened the windows and had swamped the bookshelves. It had seeped between the computer keys; drowned the rug.

Of course, Daniel tried all of his 'I told you so's' on us, but when he finally realised that all of his psychiatric claptrap was worthless: *actual* shit now, he looked at me with these terrified eyes; high-tailed it out of the room. Out the front door and out the house.

I've my own explanation though. See that doll never ate nothing but negativity all the time she was in the house. And all that crap gotta get processed *somehow*.

THE END

Further titles by A J Kirby

Bully
Paint This Town Red

SCEPTRES DE DÉLICATESSE

By Poppet

Musty brick is dank with winter. Shivering in the gloom of the singular light bulb hanging from a 1960's cord with a harness of Bakelite so brittle it looks like filigree, I brush away a veil of cobweb, shuddering when it clings to my nails.

Shaking my hand violently the sticky silk adheres better than Velcro, forcing me to scrape my fingers down the rough edge of the nearest brick to shed the white clot. Ugh.

With spine shiver I face the bottles again, blowing a quick gust to scatter the dense dust riming the curvaceous vessel under scrutiny.

Right, let's take a look at you.

Gingerly cradling it out of the rack I wipe the label, looking for the fine print mentioned in Charlie's journal.

Destillatas sanguis a morte crypta, postea. Vintage LXVI.

It's a cunning way to hide the blood of an alleged god. The dust crusting the protruding metal-sealed cork is aged to the shade of nicotine stained bone.

Lord only knows how long this has been hidden behind the clay jugs of arcana. I've sampled that, it kicked reality out of the cosmos, replacing it with the weirdest spirit walk of my life. I've been cautious with it ever since, using it only to gather insight into a dilemma. I am a curiosity as much as my wine collection.

Right, now where's that other bottle?

Counting in aramaic I skip the fourth and ninth, then count across by seventeen. The item above is the one I'm looking for.

Ah, you can see it if you know what to look for. The glass is thicker, it has to be. Teetering onto tiptoes I hook the heavy neck, withdrawing it slowly, unsure what agitating Jörmungandr blood will do. Alchemy is never as easy as we make it look.

This is man's work. I am breaking the occult laws by messing with divinity, but in my opinion we're as worthy of immortality as everyone else. Arcana is the formaldehyde of the ancients, used long before mummification became a national pastime or the birthright of kings. It worked a charm too because I've not aged a day in sixty-four years. Inheriting Charlie's relics along with his estate changed my world.

61

Always take a lover, nothing is as surprising as discovering your tryst partner never married and simply fed me lies so I wouldn't question his long absences. Why he entrusted me with the secrets after his passing is one of those conundrums better left unasked.

The problem is, I don't know what killed him. When you're the explorer in possession of everlasting life in a bottle, what can end you? All I know is the answer to that is in the pyxis which 'must not be opened'. The bastard hid the key, and it's a Chinese contraption with a hundred different combinations to unlock the puzzle as a fail safe.

It's ridiculously ironic that ancient Rome was a pedlar of Chinese products. Some things never change, the wheel just spins faster and faster, repeating the old, mingling it with the pristine until the decades blur into eras and aeons. Nothing is new, nothing. If only they'd had the foresight to stamp 'made in China' on their wares back then.

Glancing behind at the labyrinth of bottles, instinct pervades the dim corners, giving me a glimpse of foreboding. Tension tickles my spine while I clutch the vessels to my bosom with the subconscious possessiveness of a miser.

Ugh, this place gives me the fucking creeps. Pegging back to the spiral staircase I rush up the first four stone steps, the rattle of vino and sceptres behind me hinting at the angry lord of the underworld emulating an earth tremor of warning.

Ignoring the death threat the way I'd ignore a heavy breather getting his kicks by cold calling in the frigid slate of predawn, locked in the meditation of stroking his hard-on to the lullaby of 'hello?" - I hop around the staircase, sticking to the stones worn and polished with use. This lair is a regular adventure, follow the path of the ancients or your demise shall be swift and painful. Where you plant your feet determines your fate.

Weird that, how transcendental orgasm is. But why the desire to share it with a random stranger in such an impersonal way? Is it the manifestation of disgrace for inappropriately 'touching yourself'? Did mommy smack his hand away to spit maliciously 'Stop touching that, it'll fall off!' Why must pleasure be coupled with shame?

People are so fucked up. Sad pathetic psychos masquerading as upstanding members of society until safely in the vault of the night, cloistered from witnesses in a cloud of duvet peppered with stars under the accusation of all revealing blacklight.

Laughing at the image I breach the stairs, into the study where the selection of macabre and cryptic jostle for space on the ebony desk. With its hidden drawers that desk is my favourite inheritance. Obscure maps, trinkets, and amulets, were discovered in the occluded niches. Only after reading the sixth journal did I put them all back, not understanding that every shaman must ward his space from the psychic vampires coasting the ether for virginal victims.

Ignorance is a price we pay for dearly.

Placing the amphoras on the table at the hearth, I plop into my chaise longue which smells of Poison while temptingly addictive while skating naked soles over the midnight velvet. The sensuality of velvet on nude skin is vastly underestimated. That sounds like a painting by Van Gogh or Gauguin, *Velvet on Nude*.

Smiling at the thought, I fidget, waiting the allotted time.

The sealed neck of the *Destillatas sanguis a morte crypta, postea* begins to ooze silver rivulets down the warped glass. Silver tears with the viscosity of mercury are mesmerising to observe. Oh how I've learned about glass in my time in this manor. Fascinated by the gallium metal melting at room temperature, I'm lost in the mental realm of Vikings having distinct panes of glass for decoration and windows before Christ was even born, staining it with minerals the way mediaeval painters made their own alchemy by grinding lapis lazuli and mixing it with tallow and egg yolks.

The liquid mirror of gallium is now pooled in the smoky-quartz ashtray and I dare to lift the coveted bottle now that the hermetic seal has liquefied. Uncorking the fragile stopper, I sample a whiff.

Sniffing the blood of 'god', the hint of citrus doesn't instil me with any measure of confidence. I think old Charlie got ripped off on this one.

Inserting the dropper, I suction a thimble measure out of the reservoir, dripping it into the waiting chalice drop by precise drop. The chalice is Odin's horn no less. I sometimes think alchemists were bored, so they complicated their lives endlessly by changing names and convoluting recipes.

Peeling the vellum off the neck of my second acquisition, I repeat the process with the serpent blood which will be the demise of Odin when Armageddon merges the dimensions between god and man. It was all mythology to me until sampling arcana, and then I was born again, a devout acolyte in the shadowlands of the 'overactive' imagination.

The gnosis of the ambrosias I've sampled have endowed me with many attributes most women would give their left ovary for. Including the ability to perform magic more arcane than the hoodoo Moses practised.

There is no veil between god and man when man consumes the abilities of the gods by assimilating their blood within his own organism, born to die but preserved in a state of euphoric stasis.

Adding the philosopher's stone grinds to the horn, I sit forward with anticipation at the effervescent fizz congealing the potion of Jörmungandr Serpent and Christ. The philosopher's stone is not half as enigmatic as literature would have you believe, it is the stone owned by the archangel Michael.

Biblically sanctioned it is carbuncle. Carbuncle thwarts Drako's toxic blood, stare, and venomous fangs – yet it is accredited the unique property of fire, burning through thine enemy like the fiery swords of Eden. It is merely homeopathic, like cures like.

It's all a riddle to addle the ignorant, it is simply a ruby without fractures or flaws, the kind employed for laser surgery, how very vague the bible is calling it a sword of fire. It makes me ponder if the ark of the covenant housed diagrams to construct weapons of diabolical destruction. A discerning mind can identify the practical logic inside the esoteric ramblings of a scribe.

It seems excessive to add ruby dust to the potion, but I'm not about to mess with perfection. Not when within my clammy grasp is immortality.

Relaxing back I lift the horn, apprehension knotting my stomach as I become the guinea pig for theory. Bottoms up Charlie, this one's for you.

My newest will and testament is on the desk lest I meet my fate from guzzling the resurrected and the reaper in one foul gulp.

But then surely the carbuncle will apprehend the dearth delivered by basilisk venom? Too late for regrets.

It's thicker than curdled whey and the cathartic reaction is like swallowing spunk for the first time. The gag reflex at something warm and coagulated is instinctive and I squash my hand over my lips, forcing the soured sacr noir down my gullet the way an alcoholic swallows his own vomit, simply washing it down with a palate cleansing shot of moonshine while hoping no one noticed his chipmunk cheeks.

I should have prepared a chaser, this is vile.

My mouth and eyes water uncontrollably while my vision distorts to the epic doodles of Dali. Slumping heavily while my pulse percussions erratically, my limbs become fluid and the room fills with phosphorescent water.

The hearth dances a frenzy; fire applauds in loud snaps when the flames leap up the flue. Resins dissolve into gold and opal, highlighting the formidable shadow jaunting across the creaking mahogany floorboards to leer over my prone form.

The primeval supervisor has eyes darker than hematite, eerily glistening the portals to hinterlands. It's obscene when the face solidifies, the chasm of his mandibles widening to plunder the taste off my tongue, relishing the panacea as if it's his own personal elixir.

Floating on the sublime high of the abyss, it reminds me again of the zen delight of orgasm's meditation, suspending reality for millennia, even longer if you're distilling E in your bloodstream. This is like it, but better, oh my god it's so much better.

I've no doubt the shadow is a hallucination. I'm coherent enough to logically explore the circumspect. The libation of paradox is likely what the grail is. Shit! Did I just drink the holy grail?

But it's decadent, divine, an aphrodisiac that simmers the blood until you're compelled to masturbate. It's conscription to pleasure, mentally, physically, spiritually, the water warm and tender, tracing hot bubbles up my legs to pop in pixie kisses on rigid flesh alive with the seizures of desire.

Delirium smothers lucidity and I swoon in the black arms of a cremated friend. Panting, my heart having spasms while the metamorphosis controls my organs, the ring on his left hand garners study. It's the sigil of my swain.

"Charlie?" I gurgle through the oceanic prism.

"Sorry love, I knew you'd do it. Won't be long now," he murmurs, holding vigil over my quietus.

Why? Why lie? Why pretend you're dead and wait seventy years before showing yourself?

"You haven't aged a day over thirty-two," I accuse the effigy of the demised. My voice distorts as if I'm gargling celestial melodies.

The hypodermic needle is the vast kind used to baste Turkey at Christmas, and I balk when the spike enters my arm with the sensitivity of Mjölnir.

Morbid fascination seizes my attention as I blithely observe him withdrawing my blood with the interest of a third party watching an autopsy.

The pyxis that may not be opened is deftly exposed under his sure touch, nimbly withdrawing a vial, injecting my life force into the sanitary confines.

"Why?" I warble, the room becoming awfully dark.

"Only a female can ingest them both and create the remedy for life's termination. Don't take it personally darling, you're simply a means to an end."

Isn't that an ironic statement.

He gives me a mordant smirk, and I wonder how long I've lived inside his home dreaming of his kisses and penetration while under the influence of his hallucinatory hookah, and it was really him? Every delusional coitus was an illusion.

"It mirrors life, Angela. There's no way to separate delusion from illusion unless you have the eyes of Horus."

The all seeing eyes flare in the distance, his face at the end of a long constricting vein, the stare of my lover, the last vice to drive me insane.

Succumbing to the agony, oxygen depravation bleeds the last drop for his nefarious apothecary.

Pandora's petite chest of diabolical magic is resealed, housing tiny ampules of everlasting life. One drop on the tongue administered twice a day, for eternity... the dose was in the final journal. I can see now that the supply must be replenished on occasion.

Hindsight always has clarity greed smudges. Never underestimate the lengths an alchemist will go to in his quest to master his elements.

A means to an end, the holy grail... in the end it is me who's frail, except for one minor point Charlie.

As a precautionary measure I always keep a disc of phoenix ash adhered to my palate. In sixty-three hours I will hunt you down and cut out your heart.

Then you shall become my Sceptre de Délicatesse, daaarling.

Touché motherfucker.

Touché.

THE END

Further titles by Poppet

Darkroom
Satanarium (Darkroom Saga Book 2)
Over Exposure (Darkroom Saga Book 3)
Wrapture (Darkroom Saga Book 4)
Quislings
Dusan
Penance

WAITING …

By Ricki Thomas

It was a gift from up high, the view from his bedroom window, the temptress who would sit on the step by the back door, cigarette in hand, five or six times every evening, and many more times during the day. For three months now she'd sat in pyjamas and dressing gown, puffing on her addiction, oblivious to the interest she caused in the house directly behind her own.

Tonight, though, he was braver. Tonight he wanted to show her his jewels. In the darkness he took off his clothes and stood before the glass, curtains wide, his manhood displayed for her to lust after. In his mind she was admiring his masculinity; in reality, the night showed her a black veil. She took a final drag and threw the butt onto the overgrown lawn, locking the door behind her as she returned to the safety of her home.

"I don't know why, but I always feel like someone's watching me when I go out the back." Barbora had two friends with her; they'd brought a bottle of her favourite Babicka vodka and two hundred Vicomt cigarettes, purchased on the recent trip to their homeland. Karel laughed; Barbora was always dramatic, anything to get an audience.

Dušan, however, wasn't so flippant. "We'll go for a smoke now, we can have a look around the garden and make sure nobody's out there. If nothing else, it'll put your mind at rest."

With their drinks they stepped outside, the frosty air biting their cheeks and noses, and Barbora sat on the step as she always did, leaving her companions to stand, stepping from one foot to the other, shivering against the cold. "Can't you feel the eyes on you?"

Karel chuckled derisively. "It's your imagination."

What a bitch. What a disgusting, vile slag. Not one man, but two, parading her conquests in front of him, flaunting her sexuality. He stared through the glass, jaw clenched in anger, and he wanted to drag her from the step, grind the burning cigarette into her skin, her eyes, her blood red lips. How dare she taunt him? She was going to pay for this, and it would be nothing more than she deserved. He would wait, he had enough patience, and he would strike when he knew she was alone. In the meantime, he would plan his assault, every detail from the stealthy approach to the moment of death.

There had been no particular reason for Barbora to emigrate from her country, no war to escape, no stories of torture to relate; she'd simply not liked her life, the scrimping and saving of her family, their tears and depression, and friends who had relocated successfully told her that finding work was easy. Emotionally, physically, and mentally strong, she'd moved from the world she knew to one of hope.

It had been a smooth process, the journey into the unknown, and within months she'd settled into a shared house and secured a steady job. Discovering the country so different from her own was exciting, filling her mind with tales to send home in the rare letter she begrudged her mother, and she loved the lifestyle and security.

But her plan had backfired when the friends she'd moved in with had left her, high and dry. Unable to find replacements to fill the spare bedrooms and help with the bills, she'd fallen disastrously into debt. Her life had become monotonous, a dreary existence of unending overtime to earn money, and the stress had eventually proved too much; she'd cracked and given up, begging a doctor for some tablets and a sick note. Now the days rolled into one, mornings avoided in the comfort of her bed, afternoons wasted with meaningless television, evenings drowned in alcohol.

Somewhere deep inside, a weak voice insisted that her luck would change, that somewhere, somehow, she'd find steps to lead her from the chasmic hole she'd fallen into. That was all that stopped her from ending it all; from stepping into the noose that hung in the bedroom cupboard for the day she couldn't cope anymore.

"You're just being silly; you think too much." Karel gave her a fleeting cuddle, a comforting pat on the back once she'd passed him some money for the supplies he'd furnished her with.

"Do you think the same?" She was pleading, her fears belittled.

"I didn't see anyone at the windows, nothing suspicious. Just keep the door locked when you're inside, and try not to worry. You've got my number if anything happens, and there's always the police."

"Thanks, Dušan." She hugged him, grateful for his kindness and understanding, and watched the two men walk away.

Over his shoulder, Dušan reassured her a final time. "Why don't you smoke out the front if you're really worried?"

"Karel's right, I'm just being stupid. I'll get a dog, or something."

His rage was physical, hands balled to fists, face reddened, muscles tensed all over his body. The barefaced cheek of that slut, taunting him, laughing at him. For months he'd coveted her, imagined her slender legs spread for him, begging him to use her as he pleased, to slice her skin and make her bleed, to wail in pain as he bit her breasts and forced himself inside her. He checked through the window again to see if she was back, but the step was empty and the door closed. Growling with frustration, he punched the wall.

Barbora hadn't wanted to share the bottle she could barely afford, she'd only allowed the men a small measure each, but as soon as they left she poured some into a large tumbler, diluting it only slightly with some cola, and knocked it back. It burned the back of her mouth, the taste bitter and harsh, but that didn't stop her from repeating the process. With no other solution to her ridiculous worries, she gave herself a pep talk, repeating the mantra that Karel was right. Her imagination had always run rampant, the product of a creative mind, and the notion that some pervert would sit at a window, only waiting for her to have a cigarette? Pure nonsense.

Her bravado fuelled with alcohol, she poured another and unlocked the back door, showing the world she was afraid of nothing; if she wanted to smoke in her own back garden, then she would. She took a stick from the pack, her fifth of the evening, and inhaled deeply as she lit it, savouring the harsh strength.

Breathing out, she glanced around. As always, several neighbours were still awake at the late hour, their lights gleaming through curtained windows. There was nothing untoward to see, nor hear, and she wrapped her dressing gown tightly around her, the chill in the air biting as the evening dew turned slowly to frost on the ground. Gradually growing less vigilant as her mind blurred further, she sipped her drink and smoked another king-size. There was nothing to worry about.

He could only hope that the two cigarettes hadn't been the last of the evening; that she hadn't retired to bed without giving him a chance to avenge her for her vices. The wind had picked up over the course of the evening and was freezing his fingers, despite the gloves, as he waded through the grass, cloaked completely in black to avoid prying eyes. The streetlights glowed between the houses, but if he stayed by the fence, silent, in the shadow of the brick shed, detection was unlikely. It was now a waiting game, a testimony to his patience, and it was possible that she'd go to bed without returning for a final smoke, but if he couldn't have her tonight, then there was always tomorrow.

Every now and then he peeped from his shelter, checking the lights that shone through the windows, knowing that as long as they were on his chance may still come. Eventually the kitchen lit up, and adrenaline began to pump through him, anticipating the joy of holding her at last, making her pay for teasing him for so many months. He could hear the tart's voice in his imagination, begging him for mercy, and he gripped the knife tightly as he became aroused.

The key sounded in the lock and Barbora stepped through the door, closing it behind her to stop the smell of tobacco wafting into the house. As a precaution she glanced left and right, scanning the garden to ensure her safety and, relaxed, she lit the cigarette and sat on the cold step, damp with frost.

A shuffling sound alerted her and her eyes darted back and forth, part of her sure she was being dramatic, the other half urging her to run inside to safety. She took a swig of her drink, calming herself, berating herself, and forced herself to relax. There was nobody there.

With a surge of courage he knew the moment was perfect; with the surprise of his presence he would take advantage of her confusion. Wielding the knife he burst from the shadows and lunged towards her. The tumbler fell from her hand and smashed on the step, her body too slow to retaliate as he landed on her, knocking her sideways. The weapon pierced her clothes easily, the sharpened blade slicing through her olive skin and meeting her insides.

Wanting to scream, to shout for help, her mouth was muted, tongue lame with shock. The blows felt like punches, but she could tell from the blood that rhythmically sprayed from her abdomen that they were more than that. There was no recognition, her attacker a stranger, and her inebriated mind remained dumb to why he'd chosen her for his murderous frenzy.

The woes of her pointless depression disappeared as she valiantly fought for the life she hadn't wanted, swinging her arms wildly, kicking the man whose eyes were deep hollows, as he raised his hand again and again, repeatedly forcing the blade back inside her. There was no pain, just an overwhelming incomprehension, and she felt her fight leaving, ebbing slowly away as her fuzzy mind darkened.

He watched her body fall, pink nightwear torn and scarlet, and he carefully scanned the garden to ensure there were no witnesses, that a vigilant neighbour hadn't heard the commotion and come out to ruin his exhilarating attack, but the world was stilled; there was no audience.

He knelt beside her and spread her legs, exposing the filth of her prostitution, and he cut, mutilated, to absolve her in death of her crimes in life. He wanted everyone to know when they found her spent body that she was a whore, the scum of the world, and he uncovered her bosom, plunging the knife into each breast to release her vileness and leave her in peace.

The shock and disgust of Barbora's death reached far and wide, filling the newspapers with suppositions and slurs, blaming society, politics, police, and the victim herself, but the fuss died down as new events took precedence; the killer remained unfound.

He basked in the thrill of his foray into murder, each frenzied step burned in his memory to relive as he pleased, and he knew that once would never be enough. The terrified eyes pleading, face scrunched in confusion, the power of choosing her death over life; he was invincible, he was chosen, and the only thing that would stop him now would be incarceration or his own demise.

He glared through the window at the latest whore in her garden, shamelessly hanging her washing after dark, and he knew she was out there purely for him; it was obvious in her eyes. It wouldn't be today, he just wasn't ready, but one day she'd give him a sign and he'd be prepared, the approach and escape route plotted, and he would take her tawdry life to exonerate her sins, just like he had with Barbora. It was just a matter of waiting.

THE END

Further titles by Ricki Thomas

BEST OF SHOW

By Asher Wismer

Dear Mother:

When I was thirteen, Dad died. That year, your roses won Best of Show in the annual Horticulture Fair.

You always entered your flowers. You grew dozens, millions of shades and hues, always sending away for exotic plants and seeds (oh, God, the Phalaenopsis Orchid from Hawaii, never could sprout here, too cold, but you made it work, built a little greenhouse in a windowbox and hell if it didn't bloom, not good enough to win but everyone complimented you on it....)

You never won anything before; best you could hope for was a condescending smile from the judges, and in the best of times, when you entered the horrible Clematis florida Sieboldii, a solid discussion of how skilled you must be to have cultivated this particular plant in our frigid climate.

We moved once, after that, trying (I think) to get away from the bad memories, but the mortgage pushed us too far into the red, and your job went belly up in that mini-recession, and they gave us a good deal on our old home -- it still bugs me, they must have lost so much money on that deal, and sometimes when the sun shines I think that maybe they kept the house for us because they knew that we couldn't make it in the city, that out of the goodness of their wizened little hearts they gave us that deal to help us get back on our feet.

Other times, I think they couldn't sell the shithole place to anyone else.

When I was fifteen, working in the factory and making just enough money to help with winter heating, my sister -- your daughter -- slipped on the ice and broke her neck. The doctors told us it was a freak accident, girl her age dying on a simple slip, the angle just right to separate the spinal column at the base of the skull. In the winter cold, death came in seconds; our only consolation was that she couldn't feel anything after the spine separated... it would have been painless.

Only who gives a shit? Painless isn't goddamn good enough, you understand? Because that was just what we needed, the funeral costs and the pity of the neighbors, and that was the only year in my life that you didn't enter any flowers; couldn't afford the time to cultivate them, prune them, make them pretty enough for those fascist judges with their little ribbons. You worked her fingers down to the bone for our education, and sure, now there was a little more money to spread around.

No fucking consolation, that.

'Course, that winter was one of the hardest we ever had, snow up to five feet in drifts, and I never saw the front yard till the summer thaw. By that time, there was no connection.

Moneywise, things got a little better over the next few years, and I took a slightly more lucrative job in the city, short commute but worth it in the long run, and you could relax a little bit. That year, you entered some bizarre nightmare of a plant from Africa, and I never did figure out how Best of Show went to some old bitch's stinking pumpkin.

A pumpkin, for God's sake.

Do you have to take a course in Dumbass Cum Laude to be a horticulture judge?

I tried to get help for you, really I did. The crying got worse, the apathy, the pure misery. It hurt, hurt you, hurt me to watch it; no solace for the victim, not here, not in reality. I graduated late, got a better job, now you didn't have to work at all, with just the two of us living there in that empty house, and I didn't dare move out because I was afraid that you would get too depressed.

You know what I mean, right?

I had started to get a life, to socialize around town, and then something went wrong in your head. Not like you'd been playing with a full deck all along, you understand, but this was worse. You thought I was abandoning you, going off and leaving you to die alone with nothing and no one, and I was just staying out a little later than usual, but you tried to kill yourself over it.

Is it becoming more clear?

It was worse than anything I could ever imagine. Just when things were starting to go well, I was making enough money to keep us alive and putting a little bit away for the future, and all this because I dared to have a beer after work.

The blood was so red on your wrists, and it was by the grace of god (hell, by the grace of the devil himself, is what I really think) that I got to you in time, made you drink, put pressure on the cuts until they began to scab in the fabric of the shirt that I had torn right off my back.

It wasn't enough for you, though. Somehow this was still my fault. But before I could really get all this through my head, we got the black-bordered card from the lawyer's office, and it really was by the grace of god that you were still so doped up that my uncle's death didn't send you

73

completely off the bend. You stayed in the hospital for a month; I made them keep you there on suicide watch, and for that month I had peace, but I also started to figure out what was going on. It was the middle of summer, hottest one in my lifetime, and the soil was baked dry everywhere. Nothing was growing... and that's how I made the connection.

Not that it'll help in the long run, and heaven knows that it won't help me, but I have a feeling that maybe I should have stayed out a little longer that night, not got back home so fast. Maybe I should have let you die, because now I'll never be free. And you know what? It took me forever to figure it out, that there was only one thing that ever made you happy.

So that's why I'm doing this. I don't think you'll understand, Mother, but on the off-chance that you do, here's what the deal is. Those roses in the front yard? The ones that only bloom once in a while, and that I've mown over a hundred times but they always come back? The bush lives but the they only bloom when someone in our family dies.

I don't know why, I don't know why us, why not some other people, but the fact is that every time one of us dies they bloom like the blood of an angel. They could possibly be the most beautiful flower I've ever seen, and is that just because I've grown so used to associating them with our deaths? You'll be ok, after, because of the insurance, I took care of the whole thing. After that, it's up to you; I've done everything I can.

It doesn't matter. Because you've been so sad, crying, I couldn't make you happy no matter how many seeds I bought you or how many of the nicest girls in town I told you I would get with because you told me I needed a nice girl, even though none of them could be good enough, especially if they took me away. I couldn't do anything right, but I can do this for you.

The roses will take a week to bloom, just in time for the Horticulture Fair. You can enter them and maybe you'll win Best of Show again, who knows, but they'll all look at the flowers and they will envy you, Mother, they will be salivating for those roses, nobody else ever had such beautiful roses as the ones that bloomed after Dad died.

THE END

Further titles by Asher Wismer

Holiday of the Dead

HAPPY NOW?

By David Rogers

Here it is: I've missed you. God, just saying that makes me feel lighter. I've denied myself this comfort for too long. I've missed you. Yeah, those words are solid.

The windshield acts like a magnifying glass and I am being cooked. The ocean makes shushing sounds as it tries to cancel out all the noise between my ears and isn't that kind?

I consider keying the ignition and inching my foot down until we buzz from the edge as some sort of demented metal insect.

I want to leave behind fire. I want to twist a steel sarcophagus around us.

Birds fly high above but what's the point. Down there, rocks wait. Down there are the creatures that will turn our bodies into temples. I want them to eat out our eyes and furnish our innards with eggs. I want them to drag life back into each of us.

I start the car and it chokes on its own smoke. Your vibrations rattle through its frame just as they throbbed upon the layers of distance that you put between us.

As we fall I'll think about the saltwater that will rot away our top layers and how my body would float if my heart wasn't so goddamn heavy.

I'll think about how moonlight once picked out the nuts of your bones; the ridges of your spine contorted with ecstasy.

We've come a long way. I squint against the light and trace the horizon with the tip of my finger. The border of the world is a sad face. I stick out my thumb and blot out the sun with it.

The seatbelt clicks into place and I retch on an unexpected hairball of laughter when I realise how ridiculous I'm being.

I yield to the bitterness of tears when they are tipped into the upward crevice of my mouth. For a moment, my mouth is the horizon but inverted.

I remove the seatbelt and gather the steering wheel up in my wet hands. I tease the accelerator and I make our coffin purr.

It dry-heaves forward.

Here it is: a blunt conclusion.

The end of the world creeps closer until the front of the car dips down and its windscreen fills with an effigy of cool blue water and grey sand.

We tip until the grip we have is only on the concrete air.

The rocks gathered at the base of the cliff are thrown towards us. My tie flops like a tongue onto the steering wheel.

Loose change, empty bottles and a stuffed animal tumble to the front of the car. I look into the dead black eyes of the little red elephant then down at the baby in my lap.

I twist the dial of the radio and out pours a cushion of static.

I groan as we fall and here it is, here it is: God, Kim. I'm so sorry but I can't live without y–

THE END

Further titles by David Rogers

Somewhat Damaged

EVERYTHING MUST GO

By Kirsty Neary

We should have known the dirty fucker would wind up in the Gorbals. Only Glasgow's finest ghetto would do for the likes of its schemes, tricks, feints and filthy backhanders – not exactly unfamiliar territory for those kinds of goings-on, except for two crucial things It had that the others did not: pure, unadulterated junk of a vintage no other dealers could ever hope to match, and by now, an unchallenged monopoly. We'd tried so hard to evade It, circling back on ourselves and jumping through loops all over the goddamn city, but it was no use. Not by now, not for a long time, if we were being honest with ourselves instead of trusting to junkie logic. Swallowed pride eased by Its' product, our honey-glazed veins dribbling for more of the same, we knew we'd have to come looking for It in the end.

The Fiend.

So, from Partick through the city centre we'd come, to the prefab vertical slums the Council liked to pretend had never existed. It looked like we were all in for bit of a homecoming.

Shame it lacked a pop of the local Aldi's answer to the fizz posh West End cunts drank, especially since we'd been tracking it to the South Side all fucking day. Grant stopped to catch his smokers' breath, choking a mouthful of phlegm over the bridge into the Clyde.

'Grant! Move it! We kin still *smell* the bastard.'

He shook his head, scattering tobacco over a Rizla. Fetid wind peeling off the river made this an exercise in time-wasting, but that's what folk like us *do* in a crisis – whack out the smokes, nip from the hip flask, kidding on we're *stopping to think*. I leaned back into the weather-bitten bridge, chiselling further dents in a spine already buggered from traipsing the city.

'Whit d'ye 'hink it's lookin' fir?'

Grant shrugged.

'Same's the rest ay us, Cath,' he replied, syllables going awry as he picked flecks of snout from his lips. 'A safe hoose. The Fiend's loaded: needin' somewhere tae hide oot an' count the pennies.'

'Least *someb'dy's* dain' awright fir themsels, eh?' Need's strain coated my tongue like bargain-bin linctus. I eyed the roll-up and, clock-worked, Grant handed it over and drew another from behind his ear. Plus points

77

when on urban safari: a witch doctor's touch with the baccy, even if a fag's nowhere near enough to take the edge off.

A minute's static smoking permitted a stretching of ribcages and catching of breath between wheezes. Circumstances aside, it's nice to get a wee tour-bus angle on the river. Peel eyes off the drink-sticky pavements, ignore ankle-depth garbage, you can almost pretend you're overlooking one of those European beauties holiday-packaged on the back of the Sun. Riverboat Casino lights stipple the tide with bright buds, sent swimming downriver like neon confetti. Even sunset here can still be an event if you squint or have enough of a drink in the system, the sky a wedge of watermelon pre-sliced by high rises and telly masts, pigeons a crazed jittering of seeds as they homed in on last nights' takeaways' saturated fat and hieroglyph additives.

But enough.

'Right. Move it,' said I, words still not quite worthy of an energy drink sponsorship, desperation all I had left at the wheel steering onwards and upwards. Highs couched in high rises. Somebody at the City Council had a sick sense of humour, indeed.

'Do we huv tae?' Grant whined, only half-serious.

'Aye. The Fiend disappears, an' then where ir we, eh? Scuttering aboot in gutters, pickin' fag ends oot the bin? Nae chance.'

'But thir's *millions* ay them,' he groaned, indicating the limitless sprawl of high-rises, each one a middle finger of fuck-ye-ya-cunt thrust up in our direction. 'Aw they fuckin' *stairs*, Cathy. An' how're we even gonnae get inside?'

'Aw, for fuck's sake.'

I shook my head and immediately wished I hadn't, the movement clawing at the edges of my remaining high. I had to laugh, though: that the possibility of a working lift hadn't crossed either of our minds wasn't half a reminder we were back in the Gorbals.

'Used to live here masel, mind? Folks arenae as uptight as they West-End pent-hoose eejits. Bit ay chat'll get ye anywhere.'

'Fair dos,' he muttered, clenching his coat round his Biafran-wean frame, shivering. 'But Cathy, ah dunno if ah kin hold on...'

'We'll git there...we always dae...'

Wee bit cod philosophy for which we addicts are renowned round these parts. Junkie logic, but you can see it in any Glasgow pub without venturing into needle-and-spoon territory. Try it. Approach the oldest, hardest-bitten diehard lining the bar. The guy who'd be part of the woodwork if it weren't for the rhythmic raising of glass to lips, metronome-steady...aye, you could set your watch by him. Hang around and you'll be guaranteed a dribble of wisdom. Remember: these are folks whose blood's run so thick for so long with chemical lubricant it could fuel a Jeep; folks who've always, somehow, found the means even if it meant licking the floor under the boozer tables. Folks who've seen the stars exploding and decided it wasn't much to write home about. Legends or cautionary tales: whatever your take, still folks whose resilience injects a sure hit of hope into quests of this particular nature.

We held each other up as we stumbled toward the first block, our skinny limbs a jumble of snakes knotted in a basket. Past the Citz Theatre. Beckett's *Endgame* was on. Folk watching folk living in bins. Times like this, I wished irony would fuck off and give me peace.

'Spoor!' Grant cheered as we halted before shards of broken glass fanning a viscid pool of liquid ruby. No big deal: not till you've learned to carve the unremarkable to shape. 'Still fresh.'

'Good stuff, an' aw. Nane ay yir Bucky. A discerning Fiend, indeed.'

'This yin, then?'

Forty floors'-worth of stairs, and of pain. Small change next to going without, though.

'Aye.'

Further clues stippled the pathway. Piled in cairns, nothing random about it. The Fiend was teasing us. Hypo-wraps from the Clean Works project in Shawlands. Pill bottles peeled of labels. Rags pricked with bulls' eyes of blood.

'You'd 'hink the Fiend'd –' Grant began.

'– Shhh. Ah know. Tricky, tricky fucker, so he is. We're gonnae huv tae watch 'irsels.'

We stood at the panel of buzzers. Eighty names, eighty households, eighty-plus giros and counting. Folk I might know, or known, in some frame of mind less altered.

'Which wan, then?' Grant's voice trembled. Shakes setting in.

'Disnae matter. We're stood here till someb'dy lets us in.'

We started at ground floor. Anyone daft enough to shack up in such an easy B&E would be anybody's fool.

'Whit we here fir? Puntin' somethin'?'

'Awk, naw. Even the auld yins willnae let in a *salesman*. No' eftir they news stories, like.'

'So...whit, then? Jehovah's mob?'

79

'Naw, God-fearing shite's a non-starter roon' here. Strictly Prods. Wir fae the tenth flair, right? Takin' oot the rubbish an' firgoat tae stick the snib oan. Could happen'tae emdy. *Dae's a favour, pal.*'

'Fine. You dae it, but. Wummin's voice, like.'

I shrugged, hit a few buzzers, waited. Been here before, sort of. Crawling home through the street lamps' neon murk, pished, half-blind with home brew. At the front door, no idea which number's your flat, if you're even at the right building. High times.

The panel's mesh mouth spurts a crackle.

'Hello...?'

Bingo. Older voice, a woman, creaking around the edges. A *hello*, and everything – none of your *haws* or *whits* rolling from mouths still half-asleep at teatime.

I ran the spiel. Easy-ohsie, until,'What floor did you say you were living on, dear?'

'Eh...tenth.'

'And what's your name?'

I stared at the panel. Couldn't claw a single legible name from the morass of scored and peeling labels, wound up stuttering the name of my last high school guidance teacher before I got kicked out.

'Eh...Mackie. The Mackies.'

The voice box tutted. A brief old-lady giggle.

'Hmm. I'm sorry, dear, but there hasn't been a Mackie in this building since nineteen eighty-two. I'm afraid you've got the wrong building.'

'But—'

'Goodbye, dear.'

And the old bitch slammed the handset down.

'Fuck!' we groaned in time, sweat-sticky foreheads imprinting the shatter-proof glass.

The Fiend.

It had to be.

Toying with us. That's It's modus operandi – get clients so strung out they're on bended knee and up for any kind of rip-off by the time they'd pinned It down. Exhausted the fight right out of us, whatever fight remained since the Fiend had hit the city and bound us taut into its hellish commerce. Sleights of hand, ear and eye were its defensive repertoire, although these were hardly necessary. By the time we finally caught up, the Fiend could sit pretty while we sprawled like sandworms at its feet, muscles capable only of thrust enough to hit a plunger. Tricky, tricky fucker.

'So whit now?' asked Grant.

'Fuck it. Wan mair, then we're goin' in the winday. Ah don't gie a flyin' fuck anymair.'

Before the Fiend arrived, we'd have had more patience. We'd never have kept well clear of B&E, what with records like ours. Well, not in schemes like the Gorbals, anyway: why slum it when all the finest wines flowed and crisp banknotes fluttered from ripping off West End idiots too money-glazed to notice? We wouldn't *have* to. We'd already be sorted, curled up warmly in supplies on the couch, sat in satisfied silence save from the odd chuckle in the direction of the telly at what may or may not have been a joke. This, on the other hand, was very fucking far from funny.

Grant spread both hands wide on the panel, pushing down hard on every button he could reach. His arms were as bad as mine: a pleat of swollen veins, skin fine enough to afford a swatch at the cells agitating in his blood, sweat stamping inkblots on the limp cotton of his jacket.

Every time we did this, one of us would suggest we ust jack it in. That we should get clean, *live* instead of existing, arms outstretched in plea or in bliss, but of course we never do. Sat back in that same blue-flickering lounge, hands trembling, feet battering the floor, foreheads dripping like faulty taps, we always needed one more taste.

The Fiend knew its customers. It never, ever looked remotely surprised to see us again.

'Aye? Whit?' said the voice box. Very pleasant and polite the fella sounded, too – no wonder he was home on a Saturday night. Our cover story was unnecessary – Mr Congeniality slammed the handset down mid-sentence, pressing the buzzer. Anything for an easy life. Probably had a pit bull and a baseball bat behind a door never let off the chain.

We stood in the dank chill of the tiled lobby, looking up the central space between the unwinding staircases. A faithful *OUT OF ORDER* sign peeled yellow on the door of a lift in its nth year of retirement.

'Right...right...' breathed Grant, stepping on the spot like a Belsen Boxing Club prizefighter. 'Where we goin'?'

'Up. It's in here somewhere. Mind, it gets as much *fuck-aw* as we dae if we cannae find it.'

'Aye, but it shouldnae seem like so much mair *nothin'* on *oor* side.'

'S'the way it is, in't it?'

I've never been daft enough to believe what we were after was easily sourced. Whatever you didn't pay in cash, you paid in dignity. So we climbed, scouring every landing. It wasn't beyond the Fiend to leave hints dropping in subtlety the closer we got: graffiti-scrawled lyrics and quotes linked thematically by drug use (Velvet Underground, old Bill Burroughs and Hunter S. T. were firm favourites), even the odd tarnished spoon jammed into the keyhole of the very last door before the final mutual sinking of teeth into goodies. Tenth, fifteenth, eighteenth floor and still no sign. It wasn't like the Fiend not to mock us all the way, from the first pool of glass to the last grasping fist.

'This is takin' the piss,' said Grant, wheezing over the balcony of the twenty-first floor. Nothing like a wee bit aerobics to ram home the state you're in, all joints creaking for want of nutritional lubrication and buggered lungs frail as pocket-lint to the point even the deepest breaths failed to satisfy. Shrivelled hearts hissed curses down shattered veins, furious at having to work so hard in service of further abuses. Knees trembled even at rest, movement such a novelty that muscles just didn't know when to stop.

'We've missed somethin',' I said, 'The Fiend widnae let us git this far withoot another wee poke in the eye.'

'Aye, but...it was right there! Spoor! It's goat tae be here...'

Desperation crept up his throat, saying more in pitch than in words. More junkie logic. We're brilliant at it – all you have to take you from fix to fix. So, no cash, no job, rent unpaid, toilet blocked, phone cut, veins fucked, belly empty...and yet *something* would always come up, whether it's a straight deal caught on the hop or more of those fucking white rabbits with satin packets in their teeth springing from a top-hat. The Fiend *had* to be in here. Junkie logic would make it so.

'I cannae go any further, Cathy...not if I'm not abso-fucking-lutely positive..ahm dyin' here.'

I knew he could if it came to it. There's nothing we won't do, no hellfire or holy water would stop us, but we still needed a wee spark granted by conviction that the Fiend and its product were really up ahead. Still no sign, and I had a horrible feeling. Something forgotten.

'Grant...d'ye promise no' tae kill us if I tell ye somethin'?'

He shrugged, too sick and far from a fix to rankle.

'Whit?'

'Ave lived in flats like this afore, mind, an'...sometimes there's a couple ay wee granny flats roon the back. We'll've walked right past.'

'Aw...fuck... Christ, Cathy, you might ay said somethin' afore noo!'

'It wis a long time ago, Grant!'

'Aye, a few year an' too many fuckin' spliffs ago, mair like! Fuck's sake...!'

Downwards was worse than the climb, what with skeletons pounded to suet pudding now required to support a shaky descent. Pretty sure Grant was thinking the same thing with every turn of the banister – just fucking *jump,* get it over with. Finally we made it, kneecaps crumbling, powdered chalk drifting down the insides of our femurs. Grant's nostrils crinkled at the smell in the lobby, a smell I couldn't put words to other than *all wrong.* A hospital's antiseptic sterility almost but not quite masking the scent of impending death and decay; the reek of stale booze oozing from a mouth insufficiently Listerine-doused; the sorrow-sweetness of funeral flowers struggling to balm the wafts of corpse-sullied graveyard dirt.

'Fuck, it *is* doon here! 'Mon! Afore it goes oot the back way!'

Sure enough, I'd missed the corridor, half-hidden behind a musty boiler jutting its gut out into the lobby like a bouncer. Knackered, me and Grant half-leant on walls as we staggered, leaving skidmarks in the whitewash: whether in Morse Code SOS or epitaphs, I couldn't be sure, ever further from caring.

Another of the Fiend's cairns sat between two doors, one of whose name-plate matched the buzzer answered by the old bitch who'd knocked us back. Nothing too sophisticated – more bloody swabs, needle wraps, foil envelopes and dirty spoons – except for a dinky wee toy. Cheapo shit from a Happy Meal or a Frosties packet, or something, but still, a message. A green plastic dragon blowing smoke from the tip of a claw, whose limpid eyes and toothsome grin said more than any middle-finger obscenity ever could. Grant growled and kicked it against the wall, against which it stubbornly refused to shatter to pieces. He roared, stamping the daft thing into the concrete until I summoned the energy to grab onto his shoulder.

'Calm it, Grant.'

'That fuckin'...bastard of a...'

'Shhh, it's okay. Wir nearly there.'

He took a deep breath and turned to face the doors, his head bouncing back and forth like a broken doll's at the end of a spring.

'Which wan, Cathy? Which...fuckin'...wan...?'

'Goat tae be the bitch who 'members the fuckin' *Mackies,* whoever they are.'

'Go on, then. Gie her a chap.'

Chivalry and gender politics don't often come into the junkie logic equation, and so I'm not afraid of anything anymore except for going without. Clichés and ironies breed in the space between fixes, indeed: I literally had nothing left to lose. Grant propped me up as I gave the door something that began as a pounding, then dribbled to a tickle by the time the movement ran the length of my arm.

We waited, trembling, dripping, aching.

Then: slippered feet over carpet. Laboured breathing. Tobacco-yellowed net curtains twitched in the window over the peephole – and what a sight for the old bint! Me and Grant in jeans with skin-tight ambitions far too loose for our junk-sucked legs; eyes louping out like chippy pickles from soured milk complexions garnished with beads of sweat blinking as we shook.

'Yes? Can I help you?' An edge of sarcasm in her church-hall-charity-bakesale witter.

'Wir fae doon the hall,' said Grant, 'Wondered if ye could len' us a coupl'ay teabags.'

'Well, I never...how...how curious...' she said, a lightness in her tone bordering on the erotic. Obscene. I'd have thrown up if my system hadn't been such a stranger to solids for God knows how long.

She wasn't alone. We could hear high-pitched panting, nose-ward, like when you're trying not to laugh in church. It gave backdrop to a tooth-aching whiplash of a sound that conjured the image of my grandfather shaving: the slippery slicing of a cut-throat razor against a barber's strop. The door began to rattle ever so slightly on its hinges, before a shushing sound cut all signifiers to the quick. The Fiend – we *knew* it was him...her...It – beat a retreat, prolonging what we all knew was another of Its' game of Torture By Charade. The mock silence became too much to bear.

'Please, ma'am,' I said, cranking up the melodrama. It preferred clients who sounded suitably on the brink, matching It's appetite with their own desperate slavering.

'Well...okay then. I'm sure I can spare one or two.'

The usual practice being the grudging handful held over the chain, I wasn't expecting her to fling the door wide open. She looked like any dumpy auld dear you'd see pushing a tartan shopping cart along the aisles in Poundland, lilac perm tightly knotted over eyes buried deep in her crease-ironed expression, plump legs in sagging tan tights thrust into sheepskin slippers, gnarled fingers beckoning us into a hallway reeking of long-dead household pets and hospital food. And of the Fiend: wine breath, rank sweat, rotting bluebells.

'Do come in,' she said.

No. No way. Me and Grant exchanged a look. Where were the last-stand obstacles? The Fiend *was* nearby, still dragging this out. Seconds stretched hour-wards over our heads as we weighed up options that, by junkie-logic, weren't options at all. We acquiesced without a word as she led us into what was supposed to have been the front lounge.

I've never in my life seen so much...well, *junk*.

No seats, no coffee table, no telly or fish tank. No. Instead, a museum devoted to tat.

A grid-pattern of IKEA-style shelving units lined both walls. Two more took up the floor space, splitting the room into three corridors of jumble. I knew old folks were big on hoarding, but this was beyond the ridiculous, any inherent quaintness or charm back-broken over the sheer mass of junk marking lives once lived, now thick with dust. An abandoned catalogue warehouses' worth of so much migraine-inducing miscellany, it took me a minute's pause to take it all in.

My inner auctioneer identified china figurines, stopped clocks, communion candles, baby shoes, one-eyed amputee dolls, snow globes, Christmas baubles, Bakelite toasters and telephones, potato mashers and toilet brushes, Yellow Pages and Tupperware containers, empty birdcages and hoover attachments, pillowcases and remote controls, inverted cheap umbrellas and sticky bottles of sunscreen, peg bags and dustpans and more. So far, so harmless, but...I tried to and could not unsee the empty wallets, expired passports, photograph albums; the empty soft drinks bottles and confectionery wrappers stamped with long-since-revamped brand motifs, the crumpled prescriptions, the curling newspaper pages pinned to the shelving querying the whereabouts of persons last caught on camera with a full set of teeth at the age of thirteen.

Not a museum.

No. A mausoleum.

This was the Fiend's purpose-built tomb to both the confirmed-dead and the animate corpses still rapping its door for a fix. I opened my mouth to speak and emitted only a smoker's gasping for breath.

'You seem very taken by my collection,' its wrinkled sidekick chirped. 'Now, if I can just remember where I've been keeping the teabags...you *are* staying for a cuppa, of course...'

Through the reeling that foreshadows a blackout, I saw flashes of grizzled mane floating behind the shelves, disappearing and reappearing

85

like reflections patched out of broken mirrors. Grant and me staggered between the aisles, searching, pleading, but the Fiend vanished every time. Every time.

'Are you looking for something?' The old woman chewed a horrible smile between clattering dentures strung together with threads of saliva. 'I know *all* about that, dears. Put something down for half a second, turn around and it's gone...'

'Look...Mrs...there's someb'dy here we really need tae speak tae...'

'Of course you do. They all do. End up here. You've done well, but be patient...go on, have a poke around whilst you're waiting–'

'Please! We've got to–'

'Oh my, quite the mouth you have on you, dear! Pipe down – you're not *going* anywhere, *are* you?'

'No but...aye, but...please, Mrs, we can't...'

My tongue shrivelled, whimpered, collapsed in on itself.

'Everyone's in such a hurry these days! No – we'll have a nice cup of tea and a chat...if I can remember where I put those damned teabags...that's what you're here for, after all, isn't it?'

We trembled. We dripped. Ached. Wept.

The Fiend finally emerged just as our eyes blurred over. A gathering of shadows outlined only by its silhouette against air sparkling with dust motes freshly loosened. A flash of teeth bright and sharp as razor-cut speed, a flash of what might have been eyes fading to small clots of light's persistence of vision against closed lids.

It loomed. It laughed.

The Fiend.

The last thing I remember before the pain dissolved into treacle-thick blackness? The Fiend's aged puppet chirruping as Grant and I hit the floor.

'Soon we'll *all* have what we're looking for, eh...?' She giggled. 'Though heaven knows how you'll ever find *anything* without getting yourselves lost in all this bloody *junk*!'

THE END

Further titles by Kirsty Neary

The Stately Pantheon
Abstract/Concrete

HANDLING SNAKES

By I S Paton

Caleb was only fifteen, but he was the focus of attention at every sermon as he dangled the serpent above his face, its tongue flickering close enough to touch his lips. He was a slender youth, with black eyes and hair, his skin pale like a snake's belly. He was always dressed old-style, with a round collared shirt and black waistcoat. He had been preaching since he was six.

They gathered in the church, as always, on a warm Sunday morning. The green smell of growing corn hung in the air, the sky outside high and blue above the tin-roofed building. Later, it would grow unbearably hot, which is why they worshipped in the mornings and evenings. The crowds that gathered came from all across the county now, even from other states, and the feverish breathing and packed bodies added to the heat.

Abigail watched Caleb as he swayed, the snake's dark eyes locked with his own. Only the twitch of the rattle-tail and the flickering of the tongue showed that the beast was alive. The congregation seemed to sway rhythmically as well, following Caleb's example. She knew what would come next, as happened every time.

Caleb raised the snake far above his head, at arm's length. Then he spoke, in a deep voice which sounded older than his thirteen years.

'*And these signs shall follow them that believe,*' he roared, the snake twitching above his head, disturbed by the noise.

'*In my name shall they cast out devils; they shall speak with new tongues. They shall take up serpents; and if they drink any deadly thing, it shall not hurt them; they shall lay hands on the sick, and they shall recover.*'

The snake writhed, gazing across the congregation, its black-eyed glare sliding across the worshippers' eyes.

Caleb's voice grew in intensity. '*Behold, I give unto you power to tread on serpents and scorpions, and over all the power of the enemy: and nothing shall by any means hurt you.*'

The snake hissed briefly, its pale-white mouth opening, as if in agreement, and Caleb took a deep breath before speaking more slowly.

'*And Paul gathered a pile of brushwood and, as he put it on the fire, a viper fastened itself on his hand.*' He slowly waved the snake to reinforce his point. '*When the islanders saw the snake hanging from his hand, they said to each* other, "*This man must be a murderer; for though he escaped from the sea, the goddess Justice has not allowed him to live.*'"

The finale of the sermon approached, and the congregation sensed the impending climax, eyes and necks straining to see what would happen next, children lifted aloft onto shoulders.

Caleb lowered the snake towards his throat. The serpent's hiss was drowned out by the intake of breath as the worshippers anticipated his next move. Abigail's chest heaved and then stopped, breath bottled in her lungs with nearly a hundred others.

He pulled the snake tight and the fangs snapped shut on his neck, the snake writhing as it delivered its dose of venom. Caleb grimaced but stood still, before pulling the snake free from his neck and raising it above his head again.

His face was bright red, blood trickling from two deep gouges in his neck, but he continued to speak. '*And the people expected him to swell up or suddenly fall dead. But Paul shook the snake off into the fire and suffered no ill effects.*'

Caleb jerked the snake, like a whip, smashing its head open on the wooden stage as he roared, '*AND THEY SAW THIS AND SAID HE WAS A GOD!*' He flung the dead snake into the congregation and they fought to grab it and kiss it. Face red and sweating, he bowed his head and spread his arms as the worshippers roared their praise and approval. Behind him a choir of children began singing. 'You are my sun-shine, my only sun-shine….'

Abigail sneaked out early. She knew Caleb would linger round the back of the rough wooden church and she wanted to beat the throng of people squeezing through the narrow doors. He was there, standing in expectation, as she walked around the corner. The small yard was cluttered with makeshift cages, whose occupants hissed and slithered as they sensed the interloper.

'Hello, Caleb,' she said. 'The crowds are getting bigger, aren't they?'

'They come from four states, now.' His voice was proud. 'We are achieving something of greatness.'

Car engines roared from the front of the church. Some of them had radios switched on, which crackled into life with tinny music. Caleb frowned. He hated music, especially rock and roll. In fact, he was always frowning anyway and the furrow on his brow merely deepened. Something was bothering him, Abigail knew. She walked across towards him, brushing back her shining hair. He liked her hair, after all, and her perfume. She wanted to be the preacher's wife even though her parents had talked of sending her to teacher college. And there was something else as well, that made her smile, something that never left the fringes of her mind.

'Is anything the matter, Caleb?' she asked.

A cloud flitted overhead, briefly obscuring the sun. It was mirrored in her heart as she saw the eyelids flicker briefly over his dark eyes.

'No,' he said. 'No, there is nothing.'

'You aren't....seeing anyone?' The words tasted like venom in her mouth.

He rubbed her belly and pressed a finger to her lips. 'Shh,' he said. 'You are the only one. You will be my wife.' He smiled. 'I have been counseling other girls, but no more than that. After all, I am to be the preacher.' He leaned towards her, inhaling her scent. 'And I will need a wife, and a child. We will be married soon...'

As if in response, the life inside her writhed in the womb. Sometimes she thought there were twins, even triplets. She was growing, and the pregnancy would be obvious for all to see. So would the green sheen that was spreading across her skin. She relaxed in Caleb's embrace and felt the flicker of his tongue against her soft neck.

THE END

Further titles by I S Paton

By the Sword
Banzai Billy Boyle Casefile
Holiday of the Dead

DEAR MRS BURTON ...

By Giles Richard Ekins

Dear Mrs. Burton,
I refer to your letter of the 18th July, but really don't know how to respond to you'.

I looked up at the monitor. I had typed *Dead Mrs. Burton.* Easily done, the D and R are close to each other on the keyboard, the R on the top line and the D on the second line, almost immediately below and I am not a very accomplished typist. Easily done.
I shifted the cursor and made the correction.

Dear Mrs. Burton,
I refer to your letter of the 18th July, but really don't know how to respond to you. If you truly believe that your husband is trying to kill you, then this is very much a matter for the Police, rather than a Private Investigator.

I looked at Mrs. Burton's letter again. In it she claimed that her husband Eric had tried to kill her on at least 3 separate occasions. On the first occasion he had tried (so she said) to push her over the cliff at Beachey Head whilst they were on a day trip to the Sussex Coast. He appeared to stumble over a protecting stone and fell heavily into her, almost causing her to go over the edge. As she whirled and wind-milled her arms to try and gain her balance, Eric made no attempt to help her. He merely looked around to see if anyone else was about. Fortunately an elderly couple were walking a Springer spaniel not so far away, else, Mrs. Burton now believes, he would have pushed her again. As it was she dropped to her knees and saved herself from going over. She had accepted his version of events at the time, that he had not realised she was in danger, which was why he had not helped her.
I looked at the monitor again.
Dead Mrs. Burton it read again, but I was certain I had made the correction. Certain! I corrected it again, this time I making absolutely sure that I altered the D into an R.

Dear Mrs. Burton,
I refer to your letter...

90

How do you respond to a letter from someone who is convinced her husband is trying to kill her. Who won't go to the Police because she thinks they will not believe her. She had written - *'I have twice been hospitalised following nervous breakdowns and I am sure that anything I say about my husband will be dismissed as further evidence of mental instability.'*

On the second occasion that she claims he tried to kill her, Eric had insisted on ordering a Chinese takeaway for dinner, even though she had already prepared a vegetable lasagne. He went to collect the takeaway himself, even though the 'Golden Dragon' on East Street normally delivered. He did not eat any of the Szechwan Beef Chilli, normally one of his favourite dishes. Afterwards she felt violently ill, almost to the point of unconsciousness, but Eric refused to call a doctor or ambulance.

It was only by drinking heavily salted water that she was able to vomit and empty her stomach. It was this incident, taken together with the cliff side 'accident', which aroused her suspicions that he might be trying to murder her. – *'A horrible suspicion for any wife to have about her husband. It was also about this time that I discovered my husband was being unfaithful, that he had a girlfriend. I know who she is; she works in his office as Assistant Export Manager and is married herself. Marilyn Croft, the bitch.'*

I looked at the screen again, wondering what else I could say to her. The hairs on the back of my neck began to rise and I felt a chill ripple through me like an Arctic wind.

It read: *Dead Mrs. Burton.*

I felt as though I had been punched in the solar plexus. There could be no mistake this time, I had most definitely, without any possibility of doubt, typed Dear rather than Dead. But there it was on the screen again. *Dead Mrs. Burton.* My hand shook as I picked up Mrs. Burton's letter. I dialled the telephone number printed on the letter head but it just rang and rang and rang without answer. So I was no wiser than I had been before.

Words began to scroll down the monitor

Dead Mrs. Burton
Dead Mrs. Burton
Dead Mrs. Burton
Dead Mrs. Burton
Dead Mrs. Burton
DEAD MRS. BURTON.

I was afraid, I can tell you. Seriously afraid. Seriously spooked. Reaching down below my desk I switched off the power to my computer, without even saving or closing down the program. It meant I would have to re-boot when I switched on again, but I was so shaken I had reacted without thinking, anxious only to clear the screen of those awful words.

A virus, it had to be a virus, somebody had infected my computer with a virus that garbled up everything you type. That was it. It had to be. Didn't it?

I went and made myself a cup of coffee to calm my nerves, and then read the final paragraphs of Mrs. Burton's letter.

I became so paranoid about my fears that Eric was trying to kill me that I almost stopped eating, certainly anything that he had prepared or brought in. I was afraid to go to sleep at night in case he tried to smother me with a pillow – to say that I am a nervous wreck is a great understatement. On the third occasion I am sure that he had tried to kill me, Eric rewired my hairdryer, I don't know exactly what he did, as I am not mechanically minded, but when I tried to use it I got a tremendous electric shock and if I had not been wearing my trainers – with rubber soles- I would surely have died. Eric rushed in, saw me still alive but in shock, unplugged the dryer and took it away. I can only assume he corrected whatever he had done to make it unsafe. I cannot go to the police with this, so I am asking you, as a last resort to help, to prove that Eric is trying to kill me. You are my last hope.
    Please!
    Valerie Burton

But what could I do?

After some time I switched the computer back on and re-booted it. The letter I had started to write had deleted, of course, but I called up the word processing program and began again, more than a little apprehensive.

Dear Mrs. Burton,
I refer to your letter of the 18th July – more than a month since I had received the letter and I felt a terrible knot of guilt hardening like hot concrete in my stomach. Why had I waited so long before responding? The answer I suppose is that I did not believe her story, just as she feared that the police would not believe her. Even so, the desperation of her fear was so evident in her letter and I had ignored her pleas for help. But what could I have done? I asked myself, trying to assuage my conscience. Take the letter to the police myself? Possibly they might have

investigated but I rather doubt it, far too busy putting up speed cameras everywhere.

I tried to ignore the letter, tried to ignore my response. I turned away from the screen and took my cup out to the kitchen to wash it out. Then I took the rubbish sack out to the dustbin, desperate to find excuses not to go back to the computer. I had a cigarette, feeling the warm sun on my face, but then I could avoid it no longer.

I sat down at my desk again, turning my head away, trying not to look at the glowing monitor screen, my heart hammering wildly as I typed again those dread words ...*Dear Mrs Burton.* I turned away once more and closed my eyes, steeling myself to look at the screen again.

Slowly I turned towards the screen, my heart hammering in fearful anticipation. I let out a mighty sigh of relief as I read what I had typed.

Dear Mrs. Burton it read. *Dear* not *Dead.* It *must* have been a virus before, when I've finished I'll run the virus guard program again and get rid of whatever it was. Just then I heard the letter box rattle. It was the free weekly local newspaper, delivered by a cocky schoolboy called Terry Wickes who thought he deserved not only a Christmas tip but Easter, Eid, Diwali and Passover tips as well.

Casually I unfolded the paper. **HOLIDAY TRAGEDY** ran the headline and with another searing sense of dread I read on. *Tragedy struck a local couple's idyllic Silver Wedding holiday in Corfu when Valerie Burton, aged 46, drowned whilst swimming in their hotel swimming pool. Mrs. Burton's husband Eric stated that his wife had gone for a late night dip by herself. We had had a lovely meal and a few glasses of retsina and a brandy or two at the local taverna, I had no idea Valerie was going to the pool as I had fallen asleep in the chair as soon as we got back to our room...*

I ran back to the computer. Words were scrolling down the screen.

Dead Mrs. Burton
Dead Mrs. Burton
Dead Mrs. Burton.
DEAD MRS. BURTON!!!!!!!!!

THE END

Further titles by Giles Richard Ekins

Sinistrari
The Satanic Disillusionment of Charlie Chilton

NEW BEGINNING

By Troy Lambert

The light scattered the shadows from every corner of the tiny room. A sixty watt bulb would have done the trick, but Daddy liked hundred watt-ers.

"No sin can hide in this room! Lord be praised for the gift of electricity!" His bulk filled the door frame. I squinted against the light.

Daddy moved deliberately. A shuffle hindered his typically agile gait.

"You are a sinner!" he declared. My voice hid in the back of my throat. My chin bobbed in a nod.

The stack of Playboys had fuelled his rage like kerosene on a fire. There were no sheets left on my mattress and it lay on the floor, sans frame.

"A filthy, filthy sinner!" Daddy's right boot dragged on the floor as he stepped forward. It had never done that before.

My eyes adjusted. Daddy's right eye was red and oozing puss. His right lower eyelid drooped onto his cheek, his cheek drooped onto his chin. The flesh on that side of his skull appeared to be sliding off.

Something was wrong with Daddy. It could be argued that something was always wrong with Daddy. Today it was physical.

"Do you believe in Jesus son?"

"You know I do Daddy."

"Have you taken him to be your Lord and Saviour?"

I hesitated before I nodded. Usually that would have been enough. Daddy would have seen the hesitation and the beating would have begun but Daddy was not himself.

"Do you believe he can save your soul? Cleanse you from all unrighteousness?"

"I do!" I declared fearing he would not miss another hesitation.

I saw he was in pain. I wanted to reach for him, but duct tape held me securely to the wooden chair where I had slept. I could not move. His right arm dangled at his side, his left tucked behind his back. I had no idea what was in his hand.

Please Lord. I know I don't always pray like Daddy. I know sometimes I wonder if I even believe. But please Lord, don't let it be too bad. The prayer floated from my mind toward the ceiling. I feared it went no further.

"What is the penalty for sin?"

"The wages of sin is death." The answer came unbidden, drawn from the memory of youth.

"That's right!" Daddy tried to smile, but the right side of his mouth did not move.

"What's wrong Daddy?"

"Nothing!" His left eye darted back and forth while his right stay put. "Nuthink," the word caught on the way out of his mouth. When he stuck his tongue out to lick his lips he could only lick the left side.

"Who payth the penauthy forf sin?" His tongue looked larger and stayed out of his mouth while he talked.

"Jesus!" I said. "Grace Daddy! Jesus brought grace!"

"Doeth grayth mean their ith no penaulthy?

"No Daddy!" I wanted to will the punishment away and I wanted my Daddy to be okay.

He pulled his left hand out from behind his back. In it was the largest knife we had. The rusty blade protruded from the handle almost ten inches.

"You muth be punished!" He was shaking now.

"Daddy. . . ."

"There ith no other way. Spare the rod. . . ." he staggered and nearly fell.

"Daddy please!"

"Praise be to the Most High God!" he declared and raised the blade.

I tried to pitch the chair onto the floor so that he would miss. He tripped as he came forward.

The blade plunged through my right shoulder and stuck in the chair, pinning me like Jesus to the cross. Daddy stumbled as he lunged with the blade and lost his balance. He toppled me and the chair to the floor, his left hand gripping the handle of the knife tightly. He landed on his left side and rolled to his back.

I lay pinned in the chair. I could feel the blood dripping across my arm and onto the floor. Daddy was flopping around like a fish. Drool flew from his mouth and his breathing was not right. Not right at all.

"Daddy!" I tried to shout. My voice came out as a whisper. "Daddy!"

He stopped flopping around and his breathing slowed. I slipped into the darkness of unconsciousness.

95

His face filled my field of vision. He was breathing, but barely. My Daddy was dying. I struggled to move and a fire ignited in my right shoulder and raged downward, consuming my arm. I held still and the fire died to embers but I knew it would take only a slight breeze to get it raging again.

Attempting to move my left arm served as the slight breeze. The fire raged again, and the world went gray for a moment. I fought for consciousness and kept it but just barely. Moving my legs did not light the fire, but they were still fastened securely to the each other. I was trapped in a room with my dying father, and no way to go get help. For all I knew I might be dying too from a wound inflicted by the man I wanted to save; a man that had tortured me for as long as I could remember.

I lifted my head just slightly. The floor beneath it felt wet and sticky, and I knew I was bleeding from somewhere. It was not uncommon for me wake up in a pool of blood when Daddy was around. For a kid like me that screwed up all the time it was almost expected. It was my fault.

"Daddy?" I whispered. His breathing stayed shallow and irregular and he didn't move. "Daddy?" I said louder. He twitched only slightly and the fire raced down my arm and this time across my chest as well. I screamed, fighting the gray cloud hovering around the edges of my vision trying to cover me. When I screamed Daddy jolted as if startled but did not wake. I felt a tugging in my shoulder.

"Shhhh! Shhhh!" I told myself hissing through my teeth. When Daddy was angry I often shushed myself to keep him away. Now it was to keep him still. When I had recovered enough I looked down.

Daddy's hand was still wrapped firmly around the handle of the knife. Even in his dying stupor, even in his fall he hadn't let go. I started to cry.

As I did my shoulder hitched with a sob. I closed my eyes and squinted against the pain, feeling the tears flow down my cheeks. I ground my teeth together.

Don't scream! Don't scream! I told myself in my head over and over. I was trapped. There was no getting up. No way to call. The neighbours were used to screams of agony from our little house. No one called the police any more. Even if I were to scream, it would just startle Daddy. And now, more than ever in my life, I did not want to startle Daddy.

I looked around the room for anything. I was searching for the one thing I had been missing for years, and the one thing I needed more than anything else at that moment. I was searching for hope.

The situation seemed impossible. I could only see half the room from my awkward position, but it didn't matter. The floor was dusty and the corners filled with cobwebs and rat turds. The only things in the room were the chair I was taped to, the knife that stuck me to the chair, the mattress I had not been allowed to sleep on, and my dying father who was gripping the knife. I could see a couple of rusty nails protruding from the wall beside my closet. Ten feet away and only inches off the floor, they offered me nothing.

I cried again, but silent and unmoving this time. The tears streamed from my eyes, running down my cheek to the floor and mixing with my blood. I was doomed. I figured I would starve here, laying dying with my Daddy on the floor waiting for rescue. I wondered who would die first. He was a tough old bird and even after suffering a stroke or whatever had ruined his right side I thought he might outlast me.

I closed my eyes thinking I would find sleep impossible. But my tortured body took over and pulled me downward. I did not dream.

I awoke to a strange rattling noise. I had never heard it before but knew right away what it was. My father was dying. My question of who was going to go first was being answered.

The rattling was accompanied by extreme pain in my shoulder. I wasn't sure which had woken me, but the fire was back with a vengeance. The tape on my right wrist was tighter than the left and that whole arm felt like a ball of fire. The tape around my chest on that side felt tighter too, and suddenly I remembered how rusty the blade had been. Infection was the only word that came to mind.

Daddy was thrashing a little and I could feel the knife moving in the gap in my flesh. I looked down and saw he was unwittingly pulling the knife toward himself. It was stuck firmly in the chair and not wiggling free, rather I was being pulled toward him as the cut in my shoulder was being widened.

I do not know how I fought off unconsciousness. I tried to pull back away from him by tightening the muscles in my legs. I found I could almost hold my ground. His dying strength was incredible. He never released the knife at all. My dad was torturing me one last time without even knowing it.

"Daddy!" I screamed. "Let go daddy!" His eyes were rolled back in his head and I couldn't see anything but the whites. His tongue looked swollen and stuck out horribly between his teeth. He seemed to be choking on it. His face was red and panicked but he did not hear me. If anything it felt like he tightened his grip and resisted my trying to pull away. We both fought death.

I felt the knife trying to work its way loose of the wood, and had a moment of both elation and dread. What would happen if the knife pulled out? Would it reopen the wound and would I lay here and bleed to death? Or would I be free, and be able to find a way out of this room?

My body reacted without a consultation with my mind. As Daddy pulled I tried to pull away. The chair creaked and the floor scraped the skin on my right side raw as I struggled but I hardly felt it. My face bounced off the floor repeatedly.

"Daddy!" My voice came out as a roar of struggle and pain. Suddenly he stopped tugging. He did not release his grip but he was done thrashing. I closed my eyes in relief. My right ear rung from striking the floor and it took me a moment to realize silence had descended. Daddy was making no noise at all.

I opened my left eye and stared. Daddy's eyes were open in a forever stare. His teeth were closed tightly on the tip of his tongue and it was bleeding slowly. His chest sat still and unmoving. There were tiny red spots in the whites of his eyes—petechiae I think I remember them being called on crime shows. His prominent Adam's apple was hidden in the swelling of his neck.

A new odour assaulted my senses. The room smelled like shit. Daddy was dead, and had defecated one last time. I tossed my head back and screamed.

"Daddy! No Daddy!"

"Leave that kid be!" came a shout from the neighbour's yard.

"Help! Help!" I tried to shout. "Please!"

"Leave that kid be before we call the cops!" I heard a door slam, and then silence.

I sobbed. My awkward, bound position kept me from collapsing in a heap. I looked down. Daddy held the handle of the knife in a literal death grip. In death he had trapped me one last time.

Suddenly my eyes were very heavy. I felt my tears running across my face. My body was exhausted. I lost consciousness again.

I awoke to an agonizing cramp in my calf. I could not move to relieve it. My eyes popped open to Daddy's swollen face and I screamed without thinking. It took me a moment to remember where I was.

The cramp did not subside and so I tried to flex my thigh muscle to get the blood moving. Almost instantly my thigh cramped as well. If I had not been strapped to the chair I would have been fetal. But the muscles tightened with little room to move. I closed my eyes and tried to stretch as much as I could. Agony raced down my right arm reminding me my upper body was still pinned. I tossed my head and brought it around to look at my shoulder. Blood was oozing slowly out of the wound, and my Daddy still gripped the handle of the knife as tight as ever. I had no idea of telling how much time had passed but somehow I suspected that something called rigor mortis would hold Daddy and I together until I was rescued or until I died.

Slowly the cramps released. The muscles remained tight promising to return to cramping if I did anything foolish. I looked around at the half of the room I could see looking for any way I could possibly get free. There was nothing new in my vision. The ancient wood floors with my blood and my Daddy's mingling in a puddle. The two useless nails in the wall below the closet across the room. The knife stuck in my shoulder. My Daddy's face stared at the horror of death.

The only thing that seemed it could help at all was the knife. Even dull and rusty it could cut the tape that bound me. But the blade was stuck in my shoulder. The handle in my dead Daddy's hand.

Think! I tried to move my hand to my forehead instinctively. It moved a little.

It moved a little. Little movement equalled hope. Hope equalled a chance to survive. I moved my hand again and realized it could move a bit because the knife was not stuck to the wood any more. It was still in my shoulder but in my Daddy's death throes it had pulled free from the wood.

What now? I had to find a way to get the knife out of my shoulder and cut my hands free.

"Your dad will hold it for you."

"What?" I answered. "Who's there?"

There was no answer. I swore I had heard a voice speak aloud. There was no one in the room.

But the voice was right. If Daddy would not let the knife go, and it was out of the wood, he could hold it for me. I would just have to work myself off of the blade and turn around to cut the tape. Sure, nothing to it. Unless, however, you are duct taped to a chair.

You can do this, I told myself.

"You better," the voice answered. "Otherwise you're dead."

99

I whipped my head around looking for the source. There was no one around, but I swore the voice had come from over my shoulder as if someone was sitting on the mattress behind me.

"Somebody there?" I asked again. No answer. Of course no one was there. *If there was someone, they would help me. Wouldn't they?* Surely they would not just sit and watch?

I lifted my head and tried an experiment. I wiggled trying to edge backward away from the corpse that was my Daddy. I looked into his locked open eyes and started to sob again.

"He isn't your Daddy anymore," the voice said. "He's a tool."

The voice was right. Daddy wasn't in his body any more. He wasn't a great daddy when he was. His life was over, but mine was still in his hands, so to speak. I wiggled and found I could rock the chair with my bound feet and edge backwards little at a time. The pain in my shoulder was worse, but it no longer shot down my arm to my hand and wrist. It stayed put, right in the shoulder. I couldn't feel my right hand at all and I wasn't sure if that was a good thing or not but for the current exercise I was thankful.

I closed my eyes. I didn't want to see my Daddy's face. I didn't want to see the knife inching its way out of my shoulder. I didn't want to see the fresh rivulets of blood running over the dried blood like lava over the cooled flow from a volcano. I needed to concentrate on only one thing: getting free.

Progress was slow. The clock inched forward and I had no idea how much time passed. Sometimes it seemed I dozed between efforts. Sometimes it seemed like I slept for hours. The light in the room changed from light to dark and back to light again. At least one night had passed—maybe more.

I awoke fully for the first time since I had begun my effort. A fly was sitting below my Daddy's left eye cleaning himself. He had brought a flight of his friends with him and they buzzed around my Daddy's now purple face like it was an airport. The runway of his lips was busy with takeoffs, landings, and buzzing disputes over territory.

I dared to look at the knife. It was nearly clear of my shoulder. My Daddy was still gripping it tightly, holding it for me. I laughed which inspired a coughing fit. However long I had been working at this I had worked up quite a thirst. My mouth was desert dry. My tongue was swollen and sore.

"Take it easy," the voice said. I twitched with a start and the knife introduced fresh pain into my shoulder.

"Ack!" I croaked. "Who is there?" The question came as a whisper. The voice had not interrupted my struggles for quite some time. I tried to look around the half of the room I could see again, but saw nothing new. Or did I? Was that a shadow in the corner? A human shape? I squinted harder. There was something, wasn't there? It wasn't clear and I couldn't really make it out.

"You are only on stage one," the voice continued. "You have a long way to go. Stay focused."

"Help me," a whisper between my lips.

"I *am* helping," the answer came. "Now get to work."

I looked down again, compelled to obey. The knife was almost out. My shoulder and my shirt were both a mess. Dried blood was everywhere, and a fresh river flowed from my startled reaction. A few more good rocks back and it should be free. Then I would have other problems.

"Those are for then. This one is for now." My voice was a little stronger to my ears.

"Atta boy," the other voice said. I looked in the corner a moment later. Whatever shadow I had seen there was gone now.

I rocked backwards once. Almost. Twice. Just a hair more. A third time and the chair struck something. I could move back not further and the knife was still in my shoulder about a quarter of an inch judging by the curve of the blade. I tried to rock again. Whatever I was against it was solid.

The mattress. I was up against the mattress. The only other object on the floor of the entire room was against the back of the chair, keeping me from moving any farther.

"Ahhhhhhhh!" I screamed. I twisted my shoulders as far as I could, leading with my left. The knife came out.

At first I could not believe it. It was out and hanging in midair. As soon as I relaxed, it slid back in, but barely. This action did not hurt at all. So all I had to do was to slip down the mattress past the knife without cutting myself anywhere else or any worse.

And without knocking the knife out of Daddy's hand, I told myself. *Don't forget that little detail. You want him to still be holding the knife for you or you are screwed. If he drops it there is no way you will be able to pick it up by yourself.*

I relaxed for a moment, thinking. I felt very weak even after the little exertion it had taken to move three times and rock once on my left side. Whatever I was going to do I was going to have to do quickly and efficiently. I had the feeling that if I did not succeed at something soon, I was going to die here.

I looked at my Daddy and determined that wasn't going to happen. I had my whole life taken crap from him. Through it all I had maintained my love and respect for him. I had too. He was my Daddy. Suddenly now I hated him. Hated him for putting me in this position. Hated him for dying on me right when I needed him.

"I won't die here with you, Daddy." I rocked the chair back against the mattress, using my legs to "hop" it just a little as I had been. The back of the chair stuck a little way up on the mattress and then thumped back to the floor.

I knew the way now. I had to wake my legs up more than they were if this was going to work and not be another new disaster. I moved my feet the best I could within the confines of the duct tape feeling the pins and needles of them awakening. I braced myself for new cramps but they did not come. I felt the muscles begin to tire even from just flexing them to move my feet. It was now or never.

I started to hop the chair back up the side of the mattress. If this worked I would end up on my knees. In theory I could then rock the chair up until I was sitting upright. Each hop brought me closer to my knees and my breath came in ragged gasps. Finally my right knee was under me and I pushed off the mattress to go up on both knees.

It was a close thing. I rocked up on my right knee, and my left slammed onto the floor. But I had almost pushed *too* hard. I rocked up on my left knee and my right left the floor. I was going over the other way and I would land on my father's body. Something grabbed the back of the chair and kept it from going over. It brought the chair back to the balance point so I could get both knees on the floor, and balance that way with the chair still fastened to my back. Whether the hand belonged to the now gone voice or not I will never know. But I owed something or someone a debt of gratitude.

I let out a whoop and rest for a moment in the most awkward position I had ever been in. I was staring down a t a square of the floor. In this square was my Daddy's hand still holding the knife, and a trail of blood leading over to the edge of the mattress which was also visible.

Okay, now what? I was on my knees in a sitting position with a chair strapped to my back. *What next?*

"Get the chair up on the legs," the voice was still behind me, near the closet now. I no longer asked who was there, and no longer looked for shadows. The voice I would figure out later. For now I had to move. I couldn't stay kneeling here for long. I already felt light headed.

I tried an experimental rock back. My feet folded under me and I nearly went sideways. With a cry I crashed back to my knees and then forward. My head hit the floor just inches to one side near the knife. I bounced back to my knees and barely held my balance as stars danced behind my eyelids.

"Use the mattress," the voice said.

I caught my breath the best I could. I put my toes on the floor. I did a lopsided hop on my left side, and the chair moved up a few inches and stayed there. One more time, and a few more inches, although I was listing to the right. I hopped once more and curved my body to the left trying to bring myself upright. My pointed toe caught on the floor and then I was on the right two legs of the chair. I tipped and was suddenly on the left two legs. I curved my body trying to bring the chair back to balance. It landed for a moment on all fours but with the shift of my weight went backwards almost going over. I leaned forward bringing all of the legs to the floor with a crash.

I looked around, startled. Suddenly I was sitting in the chair, off the floor. Blood was rushing to places blood had not been for quite some time. My body was tingling all over and I felt extremely light headed. I was still bound. My injured shoulder throbbed. I wasn't done yet, but I was closer than I had been just an hour before.

I paused and my breath slowed. I looked around the entire room. Things were not better from this viewpoint, they were just different. I could see my Daddy's whole body now his hand holding the knife horizontal inches off the floor.

Horizontal. If the knife had been vertical to the floor things would have been better. But it wasn't. I looked down at the duct tape around my ankles and wondered how I would cut it without cutting myself at the same time.

I let my chin drop to my chest wanting to think for just a minute. My exhaustion overcame me and I dropped into restless sleep.

I awoke to a pain in my neck. It was an unbelievable cramp. I lifted my head with significant effort. The room was dark now. Hours had passed. I was no longer thirsty although my mouth was dry and I felt like my lips would crack with any movement.

"Wake up!" the voice said from the darkness behind me. "It's now or never."

"I know," I croaked.

I felt myself dying. There was no doubt about it. My time was now limited. My body was weak. It was time to get out of here if I could or make my peace with God if I could not.

I looked at the knife in the gloom. The dark spots on it were either rust or blood, I was not sure which. It pointed uselessly to the side. There had to be another way.

The nails under the closet, I thought suddenly. *The rusty nails stuck in the wall. They could cut through duct tape, right?*

I turned my head painfully on my neck as far as it would go. I felt the flesh of my shoulder tighten as I turned. The nails were there sticking invitingly from the wall. The edge of the heads looked sharp. I turned my head back.

The knife was an equal distance away in the opposite direction. The time had come for a choice.

God please! I prayed. *You got me up this far. I know I am not a man of faith like my Daddy was, but I need your help right now.*

I heard an odd clatter. I looked toward the noise. The knife had dropped from my dead Daddy's hand to the blood stained floor. It lay there now, truly useless. It might not have been what I was expecting but it was an answer to my prayer. There was only one choice now. The nails were my only hope.

Thanks God! Now just one more thing. A little strength and a little luck. Jeusnameamen. My mind slurred the last three words together at the end of the prayer the way my Daddy did. A tear rolled down my cheek as I turned away from him.

I managed to get my feet on the floor and that made the next part relatively easy compared to the rest of the ordeal. I hopped my prison toward the closet. I ended up in the perfect position. The nails were right between my feet.

I thrust my feet forward with a little effort and the nail on the right penetrated right through the tape. What luck! I thought. They are sharp. I pulled my feet back and the tape already felt looser. I thrust them forward on the nail again, and it widened the hole in the tape. I pulled back again, panting.

The nail came out of the wall with the tape and clattered to the floor. I groaned and tossed my head back, trying to pull my feet apart. The tape was not weak enough yet. Daddy did not believe in buying cheap tape.

There was one more nail left in the wall. It was my last hope. Cut the tape on my ankles with it, or give up. I shifted my feet just a little to the side to catch it. The nail caught in the tape and ripped the hole a little wider. I watched carefully and saw it wiggle in the wall as I pulled free.

I was done praying. Done hoping. All or nothing I was in. I thrust my feet forward one more time. The nail caught and the hole widened. I pulled my feet in opposite directions as hard as I could. The tape started to rip more but held.

I carefully pulled my feet out form the wall, careful to keep the nail in the centre of the enlarged hole in the tape. I thrust them forward onto the nail head one last time and with one final rip the tape broke. My legs were free.

I stretched them out in front of me and side to side away from each other. I flexed my ankles and knees feeling the weakness of the muscles. I had little time to celebrate my freedom. It was time to go.

I tilted forward and lifted the chair onto my back. I took a couple of tentative and weak steps before sitting back down. My tore my breath from the stale air around me and for a moment believed I would pass out. I couldn't let myself though, and I flexed my shoulder sharply. The pain woke me enough to get me moving. I looked back over my shoulder at my dead Daddy's body before I rose again to my awkward standing and walking position.

"Bye Daddy," I said and left the room. I rested several times on the way down the hallway. Once on the front porch.

I am still not sure how I made it down the steps. I manoeuvred down the walk and to the sidewalk out front and waited. Someone had to notice me soon.

I sat and watched the sunrise. It was the most beautiful I had ever seen even though it was nothing more than a golden orb rising into a still and cloudless sky. The air in our run-down neighbourhood smelled sweeter than it ever had.

I watched as a police car on a routine patrol rolled up. The officer in the passenger seat gaped at me in horror, and the lights on the roof came on. I had never been so grateful to see those lights before or since in my life.

That's how I got the scar. That is why I trained myself to write (and do nearly everything else) left handed. That is why I grew up early without a Daddy like all the other boys had. These events are why I believe in God and angels even though my Daddy was a terrible messenger for them.

That is why I am here today, speaking to you. That's my story. Any questions?

The room erupts in applause. There are no questions. I sit down on the stage next to the pastor.

No one comes forward to give their heart to Christ that day. But four children do come forward and confide in the adults up front for the invitation about their daddies. The police are called and four arrests are made, including the usher who runs from his place near the stage when his daughter makes her way to the front.

I smile and leave quietly. A few members of the audience shake my left hand avoiding my useless right one. Most simply avoid my gaze and my path. It's okay. I am used to it. This is my last date in Milwaukee. Tomorrow I move on to Chicago. Next week, Tampa and then Miami.

For my good and the good of all I travel and tell my story. See you in the audience? I hope so.

Now my tale is told.

THE END

PREACHER MAN

By I S Paton

On a dreary Glasgow morning, she hears him long before she sees him. A deep voice, with a hard edge, each word spat out into the air. A small crowd has gathered on Buchanan Street. Some youths mock him, gangling apes clad in football shirts. He towers above their heads, dark eyes in a narrow bearded face framed by lank hair. He wears a round collared shirt underneath a waistcoat and a long black coat. *Like a gospel rocker or a Wild West preacher*, she thinks with a smirk.

Spittle flies from his lips as he shouts, and the spectacle suddenly seems more sinister than surreal.

'WHO WILL JESUS DAMN?'

'The Book of Romans says Jesus will DAMN the HOMOSEXUALS, and the FORNICATORS, and the WICKED, and the MALICIOUS. 'He will damn the DECEITFUL and the PROUD and the COVENANT BREAKERS and the HATERS of GOD.'

He waves a worn Bible in one outstretched hand.

'The Book of Mark says THIS,' he shouts. *"And if thy hand offend thee, CUT IT OFF, for it is better than having two hands to go into HELL, where the WORM dieth not, and the FIRE is not quenched."'*

His voice builds towards a climax. *"And if thy foot offend thee, CUT IT OFF, for it is better for thee to enter halt into life, than having two feet to be cast into HELL, where their WORM dieth not, and the FIRE is not quenched."'*

His scream reaches its crescendo. *"And if thine EYE offend thee, PLUCK IT OUT, for it is better for thee to enter into the KINGDOM of God with one eye, than having two eyes to be cast into HELL, WHERE THE WORM DIETH NOT and the FIRE IS NOT QUENCHED!"'*

He slumps forward, sweat pouring down his pallid face. She walks away, hardly hearing his murmur.

'And these names shall be writ in the Book of the Damned...'

She pauses. The first names slip by, but the third one sounds familiar.

'David Smith, Hater of God...'

She shudders, but grins nervously and walks on towards work. Grand buildings overshadow her as she heads towards the Council Chambers. Her pass gets her through the security door and to her desk in the planning department. She walks across to David Smith's paper-strewn desk. He leans back in his chair, sipping coffee from a football mug.

'David,' she smiles, 'you'll never guess what I saw this morning…'

'And what would that be then, Sarah?' He is too well-groomed to be straight, but she doesn't think he is gay.

The telephone interrupts her. 'Hello, planning department, Sarah Baxter speaking…'

The day passes quickly with a dozen applications to write up for decision by the councillors. She'll be blamed if it goes wrong and get little praise if it goes right, but she is pleased with the final result, and finally hits the 'send' button, dispatching the report to her manager.

She has forgotten about the preacher until the end of the day. She turns towards Buchanan Street, to get her bus westwards, but pauses near the corner.

'No thanks,' she murmurs to herself, 'I've had enough preaching for one day.'

So she walks past the railway station instead.

Home is a one-bedroom tenement flat in a middling-to-respectable area not quite in the West End. The neighbourhood is safe enough to leave her little-used car parked on the street. It doesn't feel much like home until the curtains are drawn and music is playing quietly in the background. Manic Street Preachers, *Elvis Impersonator: Blackpool Pier*. Manic Street *Preacher*, she thinks as she listens. *So fucking funny, it's absurd.* She smiles, as she sips chilled wine and surfs the internet, thinking of the preacher man. *So fucking funny, it's absurd.*

Next day, she stops briefly at the Buchanan Street sermon, phone camera at the ready. He is there once more, a gaunt scarecrow in black, intense dark eyes staring as he yells his sermon.

'*OUT of the MOUTH of BABES and SUCKLINGS hast thou ordained STRENGTH, that thou mightest still the enemy and the AVENGER….*'

The names of the damned are read out loudly, but David Smith does not feature, so she heads for work disappointed with her mobile phone footage. Her manager Jeff is visible through the window of his closed door, speaking silently on the telephone. He slumps forward, head resting against one hand.

Louise, the administrator, is sniffling into a handkerchief.

'What's up?'

'It's David,' says Louise. 'He's dead. *Murder.*' It sounds like *murdur,* the hard consonants of television drama. Sarah is filled with a shock

108

of horror and bubbling laughter at the same time, and the conflicting emotions burst out in a sudden gasp.

The story comes together like a jigsaw. The BBC website has a feature on a man stabbed the previous night, and Louise whispers that the police phoned the office because David's number was in his wallet.

Why didn't they take the wallet? The thought sparks briefly before fading.

Later, at home, she wishes she hadn't switched on the TV. The murder is the lead item on the local evening news. Young man stabbed in a street robbery, appeal for witnesses contact Glasgow City Centre police station. *Stabbed. In the eye. If thine EYE offend thee, PLUCK IT OUT.* She curls up in bed, pillow over her head, and cries herself to sleep.

The sun is shining on Wednesday, a hint of spring in the air, and after a coffee and a croissant, she feels up to going to work. Just not past Buchanan Street.

Jeff smiles as she arrives. 'Come in for a coffee.' He turns his back, balding head and leather-patched tweed jacket, as he makes two cups of instant coffee.

'Are you better now?'

She nods, smiling brightly.

'The funeral will be on Friday afternoon. At the crematorium.' He lowers his voice. 'A subdued affair, the family are devastated.'

They are silent for a moment, staring downward, before Jeff coughs. 'Sorry to talk about work, at such a time, but could you take on David's casework? He's got one application and it needs to be sorted by the end of the week.'

She nods and picks up the file from David's half-cleared desk. *You must be fucking joking*, she thinks. *A church*. A derelict church, to be demolished for a housing site. She flicks through the file. *I'll need to do a site visit*, she thinks. She shudders as she notices the address. Dalmarnock. Less well-known than the Gorbals, but just as notorious for crime and deprivation.

It's only a short journey. The grimy bus rattles as it pulls away. The ornate brownstone buildings slide past, giving way to fenced-off derelict sites earmarked for development, and eventually the hopeless landscape of near-derelict tenements, grille-windowed off-licences and steel-shuttered pubs. The streets are deserted except for scrawny men smoking cigarettes between pints. She rings the bell and the bus jerks to a halt. The church is hard to find at first, overshadowed by tenements either side, languishing behind rusted railings and a screen of foliage. It is small and squat in the Methodist style, strangely free from the graffiti endemic elsewhere in the neighbourhood, but with the windows shattered behind metal grilles. One iron gate is hanging loose, so she pushes it open and weaves between overhanging branches and broken bottles underfoot as she approaches the scabrous wooden door, holding her nose against the stench of piss and dog-shit. Paint flakes off as she pushes the door open. With a shove, it scrapes free and she is inside.

There is a lingering hint of musty hymnbooks beneath the tang of wet-rot and damp. Her eyes slowly adjust to the gloom inside, lit only by the dim light from the shattered windows casting a criss-cross pattern on the floor. The inside is completely bare. Once there were pews and a pulpit, but now there is only a stone floor with puddles where the roof has leaked. Her eyes glide across all this, until they are seized by the full detail of the wall opposite.

It is a mural or a fresco, strange enough in an austere Presbyterian church. But this is not simply strange, it is a graffiti artwork of neon spray-paint in a childish blocky hand. The mural depicts twisted Biblical scenes, or perhaps *obscenes*.

In the centre, a crucifixion. The rake-thin neon pink body covered in a loincloth resembles the bearded preacher, crimson blood dripping from the wounds. He is grinning and his eyes are red slits.

To the right, a shepherd leads his flock. This shepherd carries a scythe and the flock are pink-naked children, crawling on all fours towards a bloodstained stone altar.

And, to the left, a Birth. The baby is crying, as are the parents, upturned faces of utter despair. Shepherds stand witness in black Nazi uniforms, alongside three Wise Men in white robes and hoods bear burning crosses.

Biblical verses are picked out in gold and black.

He shall feed his flock like a shepherd: he shall gather the lambs and shall gently lead those that are with young.

Come, ye children, hearken unto me: I will teach you the fear of the LORD.

When my father and my mother forsake me, then the LORD will take me up.

Like as a father pitieth his children, so the LORD pitieth them that fear him.

Her eyes are drawn back to the crucifixion. The cross stands behind a sky of flames, atop a fissured and rocky hill. But those are not rocks. The mound is a mosaic of interwined hands and feet, severed at the wrist and ankle, blood tricking downwards. Single eyes peep through the gaps, glistening pink worms curl around everything.

Her eyes lock with the red glare of the figure on the cross. The rest of her world fades into a haze of dots and static as it begins to slip away from her feet. Then, with a surge of will, she bites her lip and the pain brings her back.

She backs out of the church, heart hammering.

The bus takes her back to the city centre. Instead of returning to work, or even going home to rest her shredded nerves, she heads northwards on shaking legs towards the City police station in Cowcaddens. It is a concrete outpost, a fort overshadowed by grim tower blocks and enclosed to the north by the roaring curve of the motorway.

'I've got some information about the murder,' she blurts out to the desk officer.

'Take a seat, love, an' someone will be with ye.' The woman picks up a phone.

A sergeant promptly appears, bulky in his black uniform. 'If you could come with me, Miss.' He leads her into an interview room. The words spill out of her, about the preacher, about David. She can see the scepticism written all over the policeman's face as she passes over her mobile phone and the case file.

'I filmed him,' she says, 'and here's the paperwork. I'm not making this up.'

The sergeant watches the camera footage intently, staring at the small screen. Then he flicks through the file, closing it with a sigh.

'Miss Baxter.' His voice is weary. 'We've got someone for the stabbing. Keep it to yourself, please, as he's just recently been detained. But he will be charged shortly.'

'But, maybe...' Cold sweat trickles down her back.

The sergeant holds up his hand. 'Look, Miss, I'm very sorry for your loss. And this bloke is clearly some sort of nutter. We'll get someone around there tomorrow morning, as it might be a breach of the peace. But I can assure you that we have a youth in custody who committed this crime and will be charged with the offence.' He stands up, indicating the interview is over.

She returns home and curls up underneath the duvet, shutting out the world.

The next day is bright, wind blowing away the clouds. She sits on the bed, head in her hands, as the sun pours through the curtains, giving her the strength to move. She walks briskly towards George Square, letting the wind blow away her anxieties, but she still can't bear to walk down Buchanan Street even with the promise of police officers in attendance.

At work, Jeff is concerned and lingers by her desk. 'You didn't come back yesterday, we were worried.'

'Sorry,' she says. 'It was raining and I felt a bit down.' She bites her lip, chewing nervously. 'This church thing it...it feels too *personal,* too close to....what happened to David.'

'That's okay, we can park it until next month.' He does not look happy.

'I'll hang onto the file in the meantime.' She turns away towards the papers strewn on her desk, silently dismissing her boss.

The day passes in agonising slowness. She just wants it to be over, so she can escape from David's empty desk which sits in the corner of her vision like a plundered tomb.

Jeff grabs her on the way out, fussing like a mother hen. 'Are you okay for the funeral tomorrow afternoon?'

She rolls her eyes. 'Of *course* I'll be there.'

Friday morning is sunny again.

'Fuck it,' she grumbles as she sits up in bed. 'I'll see that the cops get that freak today.'

She walks along Buchanan Street. The preacher is there with his usual crowd. But there are two bright yellow blobs nearby, policemen watching with arms folded. This morning's sermon is subdued. His head is bowed forward, hair shrouding his face.

'I love them, that love me, and those that seek me early shall find me.' He looks up, imploring the heavens. 'Now hearken unto me, ye children, for blessed are they that keep my ways. And, when Jesus saw it, he was much displeased, and said unto them, suffer the little children to come unto me...'

A hand pulls her coat. 'Please Miss...'A scrawny rat-faced boy is standing there. 'I dinnae want to do it. But he'll make me.'

She glances across at the preacher, but he is engrossed in his sermon.

'It's that church. It's mental, like drugs but worse. Ye've got to get away frae here.'

He dashes away, leaving the questions hanging on her lips. She looks around in puzzlement. Her eyes are gripped by the black holes in the preacher man's pale face, he vision seized by the immense gravity, and a shiver seizes her spine. The policemen have gone away.

She wrenches her gaze away and scurries to work, where her morning slides by in a daze. No one is talking, everyone is subdued in anticipation of the funeral that afternoon.

She walks home to collect her car, driving south towards the crematorium, escaping the city for the greenery of the countryside, eventually turning onto a sweeping tree-lined driveway, surrounded by acres of immaculate lawns, shrubbery and neat white gravestones.

Hearses are queued up outside the crematorium awaiting their slots. Some services are running late, some are early, but David's funeral is perfectly on schedule.

She walks towards her colleagues at the chapel entrance, looking like a ghost. Jeff is wearing a dark suit and Louise is a Mafia widow, all sunglasses and clinging black dress. They sit towards the back of the chapel, sun streaming through the stained-glass onto the bright pine pews and flooring.

The family arrive, bearing all the shattered sorrow of a lost son. They sing the twenty-third Psalm and it is all she can do to stop from screaming as she remembers the mural. 'The Lord is my shepherd, I shall not want...' She sees the coffin borne in through a blur of tears, and sobs as the emptiness and anger wells up from deep inside her.

Jeff and Louise linger afterwards, murmuring condolences to the family, but she does not linger. She does not straight go home either. She drives north towards the city and stops at a petrol filling station just south of the Clyde. She buys a green plastic canister, and then walks back to the fuel pump, filling the canister with petrol. She picks up a box of matches as she pays the cashier for a second time.

'Hope you're not going to set yourself on fire love,' the man jokes.

She glares at him. 'I've just been to a fucking funeral.'

'Sorry.' The man's eyes seek refuge in the cash register.

Five minutes later, she is driving through the light industrial estates that surround Dalmarnock. She pulls up alongside the church as the sun is sinking in the late afternoon sky. She ignores the double yellow line outside the shabby buildings, the fresh paint the only evidence of municipal investment in the hopeless shit-strewn street. With a scrape, she forces the door open for a second time.

She does not look at the mural as she sloshes the petrol around. She throws the petrol canister to one side, then steps back and strikes a match, thrusting it into the match-box. She throws the flaring match-box into the spreading pool of petrol and darts outside.

Whump. A wave of heat follows her.

Outside, they are waiting. The preacher, flames reflected in his dark eyes, painting his pallid face in hues of orange and red, like the fiery evening sky behind him. The children, of all ages, gathered around silently on the deserted street. The rat-faced boy grins as he recognises her, his face lighting up beneath the preacher's hand which rests benignly upon his head.

The preacher speaks, his voice strong and clear above the crackling flames behind her. 'A BURNT OFFERING for the LORD.'

The intensity of his gaze holds her and all her strength drains away. The children surge forward. Meekly, like a lamb, she allows herself to be guided into the burning building. Her hair singes, her eyeballs dry up in the heat, and she is gently pushed forward until she is stripped of clothes, flesh and life itself by the surging heat.

THE END

Further titles by I S Paton

By the Sword
Banzai Billy Boyle Casefile
Holiday of the Dead

SEMANA DE FUEGO

By Jacob Rayne

'Wow, have you seen the fire?' Lyla asked.

The centre of the square was ablaze. Large packages lay on the fire, reminding Lyla and Paul of the Guy Fawkes displays back home in England.

The tour guide turned and said, 'Yeah, we're lucky to have come during what the natives call "Semana de Fuego." That translates roughly to "Fire Week." They burn idols that represent sins against their God and society.'

'Quite a celebration going on here,' Paul said.

'Yeah,' the guide continued, 'the whole village gets involved in the celebrations.'

'She's not wrong,' Lyla muttered, rubbing a hand on the Marvin the Martian tattoo on her belly.

All round the square, people were dressed in costumes which exposed most of their tanned bodies. Some were heavily tattooed, while others were covered in what looked like fake blood. They all smiled at Lyla, Paul and the rest of their tourist group.

'Friendly,' Paul said.

'Hmm?' the guide said.

'They're all very friendly.'

'Oh, yeah. You'll not find many people as welcoming as these.'

Paul crossed the square and headed for the bar area. He waited in the small queue while the barman served the remaining customers. Then he turned to Paul and said, 'English, yeah?'

'Yes. How did you know?'

'We get a lot of English tourists.'

Paul nodded and ordered two beers. He carried the frosty mugs across the square, spilling a little of the cold beer down his front. Lyla laughed at him.

'Hey, is that dummy moving?' Lyla asked, pointing to the dummy nearest them.

'Shh,' the guide said, 'they don't like it if you poke fun at their customs.'

'I wasn't, I really thought it was moving.'

'Well, it doesn't look like it,' Paul said.

'Just enjoy the celebrations,' the guide said.

They looked around. All the locals seemed to be enjoying the celebrations, drinking, dancing and watching the flickering flames.

'Ah, it's time for food,' the guide said.

A muscular, tanned local appeared, carrying a huge silver platter. From their seats, they couldn't see what was on the tray. As he got closer, he put it on a table in the bar area. The barman rang a bell and everyone fell silent.

Paul and Lyla saw a huge joint of meat on the platter. The hunk of meat swam in its own juices. The smell was intoxicating and made both of their mouths watering.

The big local who had carried the tray out beckoned Paul and Lyla over to the table to try the meat.

'He said they love having visitors,' the guide said, 'he insists that you eat first.'

'Oh, ok,' Lyla said, a little taken back by the hospitality.

She and Paul approached the table. The tray-carrying local smiled at them and carved off a thick slice of meat for her. He held it out on a grease-stained napkin.

'Thanks,' she said, taking a bite of it. Blood and juices ran down her chin. She wiped it with the napkin. 'Mmm, nice. What meat is this?'

'Boar,' the man said, 'white boar.'

He handed Paul a slice. Paul too enjoyed the meat, although it was a little too well-cooked for him.

'Nice,' he said. 'Thank you.'

The local smiled at him. 'Do you want more?'

'No, thanks,' Lyla said, her belly already full from the first hunk of meat. She sat back and tried to tongue a small piece of meat out from between her teeth.

'I'll have another,' Paul said.

The man beamed and passed him a thick slice. Paul thanked him and tucked in.

The rest of the villagers ate, satisfied that the visitors had eaten enough.

The beers complimented the meat beautifully. Paul ordered a few more. Soon they were slurring their words and giggling like idiots.

'I'm sure that dummy moved again,' Lyla said.

'What?' the big local with the platter said.

'Nothing,' Paul said.

The local nodded.

The guide wished them good night. Paul and Lyla remained in the square until the end. The party went on until the early hours. The fire blazed away underneath the mountains that loomed over the town. The scene was a snapshot of a simpler time.

Despite his double helping of the meat, his belly still gurgled. He went over to the table and asked if there was any more.

'Not till tomorrow,' the big local told him.

'Thanks,' Paul said.

'Have they run out?' Lyla said.

'Yeah. Never mind though.'

The fire reduced to embers, letting the cold mountain air through. Lyla pulled her coat tighter. They ordered one more drink and watched the fire die.

'What's in the dummies?' Lyla asked the barman.

Paul glared at her.

'Boar,' the barman smiled.

Lyla felt unsettled – the 'boars' were certainly human-shaped – but she said nothing.

The barman regarded her curiously. 'Is she ok?' he asked Paul.

'Yeah, just a little too much beer.'

The barman smiled and nodded. 'One more?'

'I'll have one more,' Paul said.

'Not for me, thanks,' Lyla smiled. The smile looked forced, even to Paul.

'So, how long you stay here?' the barman asked them.

'Four nights,' Paul said.

'That's if we don't get bored,' Lyla laughed.

Paul glared at her again. The barman smiled, but Paul thought he looked offended.

'No, there's not much for city folks like you,' he said. 'But it's our home. We love it here.'

'We do too,' Paul said, 'she didn't mean it.'

'I did,' she pouted, 'I think we'll be bored by this time tomorrow.'

'You not like our celebration?' the barman said, sounding hurt.

'She loved it,' Paul said, trying to spare the barman's feelings.

'I wouldn't say I *loved* it,' she said. 'Stop putting words in my mouth.'

Paul and Lyla glared at each other, both annoyed at the other's behaviour. The barman watched, a smile on his face.

'Maybe tomorrow we get you more involved in the show,' he said.

'Yeah, that'd be nice,' Lyla said.

'There you go,' Paul said, 'you've put him in an awkward position.'

'No,' the barman said. 'Not awkward. We like to please our guests.'

'Sorry if we've upset you,' Paul said.

'It's fine. I'll see you tomorrow…' he paused like he wanted to know Paul's name.

'I'm Paul, she's Lyla.'

'I shall see you tomorrow, Paul and Lyla. Enjoy your night.'

'Thanks,' Paul said.

Lyla ignored the barman.

'What's wrong with you?' Paul said as they walked away.

'Me? You're the one who's being all ass-kissy with them.'

'I just think it's best to be humble and polite. They went out of their way to make us feel welcome. I think we should be grateful.'

'They gave us a bit of pork, Paul. We paid over the odds for the drinks, so we paid for the pork anyway.'

'You've got a bad attitude.'

'No, I just want more for my money. This trip's cost a fucking fortune. I want more to show for it than a bit of pork and a few beers by a fire.'

Paul fell silent. He felt like pushing her into the wall. It was said that going on holiday together was a good test of a relationship. Well, as soon as they got back to England, Lyla was going to be single. There was no way he was going through this embarrassment again.

Paul let them into the room.

'And this room's such a rip-off,' Lyla shouted, throwing her handbag onto the stained, threadbare settee in the corner. She locked herself in the bathroom.

Good, Paul thought. *I can't stand to look at her either.*

He put on his headphones, closed his eyes and lay back on the bed. Marilyn Manson started to sing about the beautiful people. Paul tapped his fingers on the bedside table. Through the music, he heard Lyla shouting from the bathroom. He nudged the volume up a few notches and settled back down.

The Beautiful People faded into Ozzy's *Crazy Train*. Paul nodded along, tapped a little harder on the table.

Next thing he knew, a song he didn't recognise was playing. It seemed later. The air was much cooler and the scent of smoke had dwindled away to nothing. *Lyla must be sleeping in the bathroom*, he thought. There was no sign of her on the bed or the settee.

'Suit herself,' he muttered.

The bathroom door hit against the frame, just in the corner of his vision. He felt a little jolt of unease. He forgot about it and flicked to the next song. One of Lyla's emo bands. He skipped it as fast as possible. Another emo band came on. *Jesus, how much of this shit had she put on here?* He found some early Metallica, settled back and listened.

Roughly halfway through, he again felt the unease. This time it spread over him like ice-cold water. *I'd better get up*, he thought.

When the song finished, he paused the player, took off his headphones and went to the bathroom.

'Lyla?'

No reply.

Lyla's make-up bag was on the side of the bath, but there was no sign of Lyla. He scanned the shower for her, then checked behind the bathroom door, in case she was waiting to jump out on him. She wasn't there. The cold feeling spread through him once more. It intensified when he saw a few spots of blood by the room's front door.

His heart slamming, he pulled the door open and looked outside. He'd hoped that Lyla had just stormed out, or was hiding, to teach him a lesson, but the blood made things seem much more serious.

He ran out into the night. He wasn't sure if it was the lack of the fire or the panic he felt, but he felt much colder than he had earlier. Racing round the square, his eyes darted, looking for Lyla, seeing no sign of her.

'Can I help you?' the barman asked.

'The girl I was with, have you seen her?'

'Lyla? No, not since you left the bar.'

'Will you let me know if she turns up, please?'

'Yes of course. I'm sure you'll see her soon, Paul.'

'Thanks.'

Paul ran off. He asked everyone he encountered if they had seen Lyla. No one had. *Maybe she's back at the room*, he thought, and sprinted back. Still no sign of her. He went back out and had a good look around.

Hours later, he was no closer to finding her. He doubted he would, given the darkness of the night. It seemed all of the villagers were in bed, as the gas lamps on the walls had all been extinguished. His fingers and toes were going numb with the cold. He called off the search and went back to the room.

He slept poorly, his imagination insisting on torturing him with thoughts of various grisly acts that could have been inflicted on Lyla. He regretted watching so many horror films, as some of the punishments wouldn't have occurred to him otherwise.

He left the room early, reasoning he wasn't sleeping anyway. He asked about her again at the bar. No one had seen her. The tour guide was in the square and he told her that Lyla had disappeared. She told him not to worry; she'd turn up sooner or later.

At her insistence, he sat with her and had a coffee and a sandwich. He tried his best not to worry about Lyla, but it gnawed at him. His appetite was almost non-existent, but he ate as much as he could of the sandwich, to avoid offending the locals.

'I hear the celebration tonight's going to be a special one,' the guide said.

'Lyla's supposed to be part of it. The barman said so last night.'

'Well there you go; she's bound to be at the party tonight. I really wouldn't worry.'

'Yeah, I guess.'

Paul excused himself, leaving a generous tip on the table top. He wandered around, taking photos on his expensive camera. The mountains were breath-taking. He found himself wishing that Lyla was with him. Where the hell was she?

He put it out of his mind; it'd be just like her to be off partying somewhere while he worried about her.

'She'll be fine,' he muttered to himself.

The rest of the day passed quickly. He went back to the room, hoping to see Lyla, or at very least a note from her. The room was as he had left it, minus the bloodstain.

He showered and dressed in smart clothes for the party. When he got to the square, he pulled up a chair next to the tour guide. The heat from the fire warmed them. He watched the locals dancing in front of the spitting, hissing flames. He kept expecting Lyla to show up, but she didn't.

'She'll come,' the tour guide said, patting his hand.

He ordered a round of drinks for the table and tipped the barman, who asked if Lyla had turned up yet. As Paul carried the drinks back to the table, the locals brought out the dummies. They looked similar to the ones from the previous night.

'There are a few tonight,' Paul said, sipping his beer.

'Yeah,' the guide said, 'it's a big night. More mouths to feed.'

As Paul watched the fire, he thought he saw one of the dummies moving. He looked to the guide, but she subtly shook her head. Taking the hint, he remained silent. *Probably just my imagination anyway*, he thought.

He looked around the square. The burly man from last night approached the fire and swung one of the dummies over his shoulder as he did so. He nodded a greeting to Paul, who nodded back. Then he turned and carried the dummy into one of the buildings surrounding the square.

A few minutes later, he came back, carrying the gleaming silver platter which held a large slab of meat.

The man called Paul to the table and cut him off a wedge of the meat. It was even more tender and delicious than the previous evening's meal. Paul went back for seconds, but the platter was empty.

'Busy night,' the barman shrugged.

'Is ok,' the platter man said, 'we have another one cooking. Be ready soon.'

Paul nodded. He ordered a few beers and went back to the table. There was still no sign of Lyla. He back-handed grease from his lips and took a swig of his beer.

After a short show of dancing from some of the locals, the big man took another dummy off the fire and carried it to the same building as before. A few minutes later, he returned, carrying the platter again. He beckoned Paul and handed him a chunk of still-bloody meat.

'Just how I like it,' Paul beamed.

The man mirrored his smile.

Paul sunk his teeth into the meat, sending blood squirting from the corner of his mouth. This meat was the most flavoursome and tender yet. The people round the table smiled at him as they ate. He ate fast, eager to go back for a third helping.

There was still plenty remaining on the platter as Paul approached. The big man smiled at him and carved off a chunk. As he did, the hunk of meat flipped over, exposing a Marvin the Martian tattoo, charred but still recognisable.

The man made no attempt to hide the tattoo. Paul stared at it, then looked up at the man. The big man smiled at him. Pieces of bloody meat clung to his teeth.

'That's Lyla we're eating,' Paul shouted. The idea sickened him. He ran around the square, telling everyone that they were eating a human being. No one batted an eyelid, just continued to eat.

Paul was wide-eyed and terrified by now. He grabbed a knife from the table and ran into the roaring flames, towards the final dummy that burnt on the fire. He slit the sack which held the dummy. The corpse of a man fell onto the flames. The dead eyes stared out of the burnt, blackened face and up at Paul. Then one of them burst, showering him with thick fluid. Screaming, he dropped the knife into the flames and ran back to his table.

'We've got to go, call the police,' he told the guide.

She calmly finished her mouthful, then said, 'Sit down, Paul. You're being very disrespectful.'

'But they're killing and eating *people*.'

She sighed and rolled her eyes. Her companions laughed. 'Yes, I know. Where else do you think this lovely, tender meat comes from?'

Paul stared at her in disbelief for a few seconds, then started to run back across the square. The barman blocked his path. Paul hit him with his hardest punch, making him stagger back. Paul pushed past him and ran.

He barricaded himself in the room. Picked up the phone, expecting it to be dead. It wasn't. A card next to the phone stand had a list of emergency numbers. One was for the nearest city. He dialled it and asked for help.

As he told the operator the situation, the locals tried to smash the door in. He leant his weight against it, trying to keep it shut. Every thud went right through him. Then he heard sirens, in the distance. The banging stopped and he heard the people retreat.

He breathed a sigh of relief. There was a knock at the door. He opened it to see a cop.

Something was strange about the cop, but he couldn't figure out what it was. Then he did; the cop was the big man who had served up the meat. Who'd served up Lyla, for Christ's sake. The front of the cop's uniform was covered in blood. The big man leered and swung a calloused fist at Paul's head. His vision blurred. The fist slammed into him again, then it took hold of him and brayed his head into the doorframe.

Blood ran down Paul's face. The man was too strong for Paul's struggles to be of any consequence. He blacked out after his head collided with the doorframe a few more times.

When he woke up, he was in a building that looked like a barn. Straw covered the floor. A bucket sat in the corner, steam rising from it. He approached it. The smell of shit and piss drifted up. Once again, he felt sick. This time it was all too much. The image of the hunk of bloody meat that had once been his girlfriend flashed into his mind and he vomited into the straw.

Tears blurring his vision, he slumped to the floor. He looked around for a weapon, finding only rocks. They would have to do. The door creaked open and the big man appeared, filling the doorway. He smiled at Paul. Paul swung the rock, hitting the man on the forehead, drawing a stream of blood, but otherwise having no effect on him.

Grinning, he threw Paul to the floor. The smell of his own puke filled his nostrils as his head hit the straw. The man pulled a knife and jammed it into Paul's back. The feeling in Paul's legs abruptly cut off. He sobbed. As he willed his limbs to work, he saw a second burly man dragging in another bleeding, screaming tourist.

The man turned the tourist over and ran the knife up his front, from bladder to sternum. Blood bubbled out from the wound. Paul cried out. The big man laughed at his protests, then reached one of his hands into the tourist's wound. He started cutting out organs and throwing them into a bucket which the second man had brought him.

The tourist twitched on the blood-stained straw.

Paul felt his life ebbing away through the knife wound in his back. The man put a gag into the other tourist's mouth and pulled a foil-lined bag around him. Paul knew this was one of the dummy-bags. They dragged him out and returned with another bag and a gag for Paul.

Once the bag was fastened up, leaving Paul in darkness, the man hoisted him over his shoulder and carried him out. Through a small gap in the fabric, Paul could see the approaching flames. He tried to cry out, but the gag muffled his screams. The man threw him into the flames. Paul tried to squirm, tried to scream for help as the flames consumed him, but it was no good.

Through the gap in the bag, he saw the tour guide bring a coach load of people to the fire. They sat in the same place as Paul and Lyla had on their first night. He tried to scream a warning, but he couldn't. The flames seared his flesh. The smoke started to suffocate him. He tried to drag himself with his hands, but it was too much effort for his weakened body. He hauled himself up a little, ignoring the flames which burnt his hands. His head span. His lungs burnt with the noxious smoke. Then, able to take no more, he blacked out and flopped over onto his side.

123

On the other side of the flames, the tour guide turned to her party.

'Did that dummy just move?' one of the girls asked.

'Shh,' the tour guide said, 'they don't like it if you poke fun at their customs.'

THE END

THE STUDY IN BLUE

By Jo Reed

"It's a curious thing," Bernard remarked, "how good it is, just to talk. I can't remember the last time I was able to chat like this. You need someone to bounce things off now and then, without having to be on your guard all the time, you know what I mean?"

Colum sniffed and might have nodded, but Bernard was too busy refilling the two whisky tumblers on the workbench to notice. He raised a toast.

"To good conversation!" he said, tipping it back. Colum didn't reply.

"My father died when I was young," Bernard continued, running a hand over his thinning, grizzled pate. "Arsenic poisoning – he used it in some of his paints, to get the white pigment perfect. It was just after the affair of the 'Study in Blue'. You must remember it. The story was headline news for weeks."

He poured himself another Scotch. A spark that might have been interest came into Colum's eye, but he didn't touch his drink.

"The Study in Blue," Bernard mused. "What a masterpiece; the greatest work of the genius, Henryk Kordaly. People queued for hours to catch a glimpse of it. Guards had to be brought in to move the crowds when it was exhibited at the Louvre. There were sixty-four hidden images within a landscape of sea and sky. No one ever found them all. There were private showings for the cognoscenti. They would sit for hours, trying to solve the riddle of the sixty-four. The most any were able to find was sixty-one.

"Kordaly was accused of lying. People demanded he reveal the final three. He refused. He countered the accusations by offering a prize of one thousand guineas to anyone who solved the puzzle and identified the missing figures. For over a month it was the national sport. It is said that Queen Victoria herself requested a private viewing and sat all night with a magnifying glass, examining the painting inch by inch. It did no good. The mystery remained unsolved.

"The day the painting was due to leave the National Gallery, the unthinkable happened. The curator's account, taken from the newspaper the following day, states that as they entered the room of the 'Study in Blue' a silence fell. Someone had drawn on the canvass with black ink. There, outlined on the surface, was a set of initials; J.S.W. There was no doubt but that they were the three missing hidden images. All the other figures had been of objects – trees, horses, birds and such like, but nobody had sought letters. As the painting was taken away to attempt a restoration, a new mystery became the talk of the world. Who had managed to break into the gallery in the dead of night? How had the vandal known those letters would be there, and why had he revealed them?"

Bernard got up and walked over to the window. Colum followed with his gaze, although he didn't turn his head. Bernard opened the window and breathed in the scent of sweet peas, then came back to the workbench.

"Kordaly never painted another stroke," he continued, rummaging under the bench for a mixing bowl. "His career ended the very day of the defacement of the 'Study in Blue'. He retired to Velence, and remained steadfast in his refusal to produce any more works of art.

"My father died three weeks after the revelation of the letters. I was apprenticed to a monumental mason at the time, a kindly man who allowed me to take the off cuts home to practice on. I made a good living selling little marble ornaments and birdbaths down in Petticoat Lane. When I turned sixteen I rented a little workshop with a room above in a respectable part of Putney. My mother died a year later.

"I don't know why I decided to check the tiny attic space above the two roomed house where I grew up. It was just for completeness, I suppose. I've always been meticulous that way. In one corner of the attic room stood an easel, a half finished painting, covered in dust, still leaning upon it. Next to the easel a small table held a palette surrounded by bottles and rags. Against the wall stood a large wooden chest, on which had been thrown a rough Hessian smock.

"I wiped the dust from the canvas. It was a still life, a vase of poppies, beautifully drawn, the colours vibrant even in that dark, grimy room. Fascinated, I moved to the chest. As I lifted the lid I think I held my breath. It was crammed with rolled canvasses and stacks of charcoal sketches. I don't know how long I sat there, examining each one. I drew my fingers over figures and colours that were known to the entire world. Kordaly masterpieces, every one. I was stunned. Had my father reproduced these great works? Why? Perhaps he had intended to sell them, or even – I shuddered to think of it – pass them off as originals. It wasn't until I unfolded a large charcoal sketch at the bottom of the chest that I realised the truth.

126

"The sketch was clearly of the sixty-four hidden images in the Study in Blue. They were all there, outlined and numbered, including the final three – the letters J.S.W. I checked the others. In the bottom right hand corner of each, in a tiny, almost invisible script, were the same letters – J.S.W., the initials of my father's name – John Stuart Wardell. They weren't copies or attempted forgeries. They were originals. Every one of Kordaly's works had been painted by my father. Somehow, Kordaly had taken my father's work and passed it off as his own, achieved fame and fortune while my father languished in poverty, painting walls and breathing in the poison that took his life. I closed up my shop, gathered my meagre savings and set off for Velence, determined to confront Kordaly.

"I was only just in time. Kordaly was on his deathbed. When I announced myself I was admitted immediately. It was as though he was eager to make his confession before going to meet his God. When I reached his bedside he took my hand and wept, begging forgiveness.

"Kordaly and my father had known each other as children. Both the sons of house decorators, they had played together, attended the same school to learn their letters. Both had shown some talent in art, but Kordaly could never match my father's skill. In due course they took up the family trade, making a little extra by selling their own work in the markets. My father's work always sold well, and he was set to make a good living until one night when a combination of misfortune and Kordaly's envy brought an end to his dreams.

"They were both seventeen years old, out celebrating my father's engagement at a local alehouse. Drunk, they left, and my father accidentally knocked over a richly dressed man, who took offence and drew his blade. My father, no mean fighter, managed to catch his opponent on the temple, on which the man collapsed into the gutter. My father and Kordaly heard a policeman's whistle through the fog and ran. Neither thought more about it until the next day, when a reward was offered for information leading to the arrest of the murderer of Lord Richard Broome, found dead in the street with his sword drawn, killed by a fatal blow to the head.

"That evening, Kordaly gave my father a choice. Either he hand over his work for Kordaly to pass off as his own, or Kordaly would give him up to the police, and he would die a murderer. Out of fear, he agreed to the bargain. For the next twenty years Kordaly would tell him what to paint and my father would hand over the finished product, watching as Kordaly grew rich and took all the fame that my father should have had.

But for each painting he gave to his former friend he did another – one with his own signature – and hid it in the attic chest. The last he ever did was the Study in Blue. I'm certain that when he told Kordaly about the hidden images he didn't mention the initials. It explains why Kordaly could never reveal them.

"Kordaly had everything. He married a Hungarian heiress and retired to his native country with his wife, daughter and two sons. My father had only one child, and saw him grow to adulthood. I could have created a scandal, the greatest the art world had ever seen. But what was the point? It wouldn't bring my father back to life. It wouldn't harm Kordaly – in a few days he would be dead. But there was something I could do. Something I needed to do."

Bernard turned, and saw a strange look come into Colum's eye. He smiled.

"I'm a famous artist in my own right, now. I have all the advantages that should have been my father's. The great and the good come to me for life sized marble sculptures of their loved ones, and pay whatever I ask. They call me a genius. I don't ignore the less well off though. For a little less I fashion their brothers, sisters, aunts and grandmothers in baser stuff, so that their eyes too can rest on their loved ones, recreated perfectly in Plaster of Paris and paint. Often I have little more than a faded photograph or a seaside sketch. I can't tell you how wonderful it is to have the living model to work with. The results are so much more pleasing. Let me show you."

Bernard opened the double door into his showroom so that Colum could see.

"Fantastic, isn't it? Here we have two of my best pieces. But you will recognise them I'm sure. On the left, as you see, is a perfect facsimile of Agnes Kordaly, even down to the small wart on her left cheek and the bright orange of her pinafore. You can almost see her move, she is so lifelike. On the right, Andras, her brother, in his best visiting suit. I have one more piece to add to my collection, and the groundwork is almost done. I've already been offered more than three thousand pounds for the trio from a buyer in Kent. I have two things to thank for my greatest work to date. My skill, of course, has made a contribution, but I couldn't have done it without this."

Bernard returned to the open window and plucked a sweet pea blossom, breathed in the scent and brought it inside, held it under Colum's nose.

"Beautiful, isn't it? It's hard to believe that such a pretty thing, if swallowed, can cause complete paralysis."

He put the flower down and took up the mixing bowl, added water to the white powder inside. He stood back, head cocked on one side, regarding the figure before him, supported by metal struts, beautifully sculpted in pure white except for one small circle on the left side of the face, from which Colum's eye stared across at him in hopeless terror. Bernard scooped a little of the paste onto a small spatula.

"Almost done," he said. "I always leave an eye until the very end. I need to fill the nostrils first – I don't want that fine Kordaly nose of yours to crack when the skin starts to shrink. While I'm waiting for it to dry I can show you the colours I've picked out for your hair and skin. The image will be lifelike, I promise you. It will almost be as though you are still alive. I've called the trio 'Homage to a Great Artist'. What do you think?"

Colum said nothing, but stared with the fading vision of his one remaining eye.

THE END

Further titles by Jo Reed

The Tyranny of the Blood
A Child of the Blood
Malim's Legacy

THE ROOM

By Mark Sinclair

Time was never easy to monitor inside the room. Had it been a week, a month or a minute? He was fairly sure that it had been longer than normal this time. Much longer in fact. Then again, maybe this was part of the plan – part of the game. Although, what if something had gone horribly wrong? How could he know?

The room was claustrophobically small and intermittently hot. Hot because the water pipes he was chained to coursed with scolding hot liquid every time the heating kicked into action. Usually he could shift far away from them and avoid being burned, but then usually he wasn't in the room as long as he had been. Nor chained as hard as this. This time it felt different in so many ways. Was it meant to? Was that on purpose or was his gut reaction something to worry about?

Given that he was bound, gagged, couldn't see and could barely hear, it was almost impossible to know what was going on beyond the locked door. He knew the door was locked because he had just about heard a fat metal bolt gliding into place and resting robustly still.

That part was normal. That was to be expected. He was supposed to sit, to wait, to allow his imagination to evolve and for his expectations to grow. This is what it was all about. This was why he did this. His voluntary incarceration liberated him in a way people couldn't understand. Bound, gagged, chained, restrained, he could explore fantasy, a place where anything was possible. His consensual deprivation of liberty allowed him to feel free. The queer juxtaposition of his flights of fancy whilst manacled, tied and locked away in a suburban basement room was beyond ironic.

Normally by now something would have happened. It was true that you could never be sure what, but something would happen. Sometimes he'd be released and escorted to the door. That was all. Other times sexual acts were performed on him. Other times he was forced to perform them. Each and every time he never knew what to expect. The surprise conclusion to his submission ensured his curiosity and creativity went into overdrive. His nervousness, tension and fear climaxed in fevered anticipation at what lay ahead. Would it be this, would it be that? He never knew. The electrifying range of possibilities kept him satisfied until such time blind, bound and aroused he'd be led to his fate. As a result, each time felt like the first.

He wasn't even sure who was beyond the door. The advert he answered a year ago had been clear. He was to come into the house, strip, don a mask and wait. At some point someone would enter the room, bind him and lead him to his enclosure. It was there he would wait for varying lengths of time, not knowing what lay in store. Other than knowing the location of the house, he knew nothing of its inhabitants.

He'd been tempted to come back, to stalk the occupants and see who took pleasure from keeping him locked in such a small, hot dusty space. But what would be the point? Surely the excitement arose from not knowing. Was it a woman? Was it a man? Was it a group of people? Were they old or young? Ugly or stunning? Not knowing added to the intrigue and left him returning on a regular basis for more of the same.

On one occasion he'd been whipped. He wasn't expecting it and it hurt. It's wasn't something he had sought or would want again, but not knowing what he was due to receive, kept his interest fresh. His relationships had always been dull, straight forward and pedestrian. Dinner, dates, movies... He needed someone else to take complete control and dictate the pace. Take away his decision making abilities. Keep him guessing. He needed someone else to excite him. And the longer he stayed away from his anonymous sexual benefactor, the sooner he wanted to return.

The room continued to heat up. The leather mask he wore was not only uncomfortable but made it hard to breath. Two leather seams ran across his cheeks and rubbed against his sweating, irritated skin. It agitated him. His breath pooled against the coarse grain of the dark hide and created a searing heat. His arms were manacled to the pipes and his legs bound. A gag stuffed into his mouth, rendering him almost silent and dependent upon his nostrils for life. This became increasingly sour as he drew from the leathery pouch of hot breath for air. After a time it became unpleasant and tiring.

Why had he been left so long? He fidgeted anxiously, the leather and mental binds chaffing his skin as he sought a more comfortable resting position. His attempts to pull away from the source of the heat were doomed as he found himself anchored firmly to the spot.

Although he couldn't be sure, he knew that someone usually left him there for less time. He had read on the forums about people left for days. Maybe this is what was happening to him. Maybe this was all part of their plan. To get him to the point of panic and mania and then to spring a surprise. But what if it wasn't?

131

What if they had left the house and been run over? Or keeled over? He wouldn't have heard and he wouldn't know. He was doomed to sit and imagine. The purpose of the fetters was simple: to render him immobile and silent. Marooned in the small space in a stranger's house. If something had happened to them, he would never know. In time the necessity of the situation would demand that he got out. But when? How?

He was in a basement in a detached suburban house. He was mute and deep underground. If no one noticed the occupant had vanished who'd come looking? And even if they did, would they think to check the locked room in the basement? Would this be the place he came to sense the freedom of life, but ended up experiencing death?

What if no one knew, no one came, no one realised? What if he was left to rot. To die of starvation and dehydration. This was not beyond the realms of possibility. He thought it before, but ignored the concerns. Surely that was just being paranoid. Yet, what would happen? He was sure he'd been left longer than ever before.

What if they had gone away - left him, deliberately. Some of the people on the forums talked about being left to die, but surely they were just fantasists? No one actually ever wanted that? He didn't. He never said he did, nor that he didn't.

He sat in dismembered silence. The pulse from the pipes resonant in the room. He knew that the minute a cold blast of air swirled around his half naked torso he was safe. The door would have opened and the hot air would emulate his desire to escape the cramped space.

The length of time meant that the chains were beginning to cut, the leather to rub, the heat to rise, the excitement turn to concern. This wasn't entirely the time to panic - surely it hadn't been that long... but what if?

He tried to move, to see if there was a weakness in their encasement but slumped against the wall in resignation.

What if the worse had happened? Who in his own life would miss him? He rarely called his family, after the row, and he was out of work. When he didn't appear to claim unemployment assistance would anyone there report him missing? Would anyone notice? He'd been there one week when someone had failed to show up and they'd simply closed the files. No questions, no letters, nothing. The understanding was - if you want it you'll come. His rent was paid for a month. Even when that run out, they'd not come looking. They'd just bin his stuff and re let. The anonymity he sought restrained in a room, was prevalent in his life already.

Who'd know he was gone? Who'd care?

He knew his hobby was a little 'out there'. He knew that not everyone would understand, but it hurt no one. Usually, the excitement of expectation was sufficient to override the fears of pragmatism, but this time it was different.

Trying his hardest to remember, he felt like he'd been left at least a day. It may not have been quite that long, but it wasn't far off. The heating cycles gave the biggest clue. Usually it was just a matter of hours.

Panic wrestled with calm. Which force was the greater?

But... surely this was what he wanted. He craved a loss of control and this was the ultimate form of it. The rest of his life, however much it had left, was now in someone else's hands. He began to worry. Would he survive or would this hobby, as someone once said, be the death of him?

He was severely thirsty and hungry. The heat of the room ensured he wasn't cold but as night approached (assuming it hadn't already) the temperature would plummet. His semi naked frame would crave the heat of the pipes. It would be as if he'd been taken from a sauna and plunged into an ice bath. The sensation of restriction was beginning to lose its appeal.

He sat in silence, desperate to listen out for anything. He'd just about heard the bolt, so he knew he could hear some things. Was that a noise? How about that? The silence began to play tricks, the lack of sight failing to enhance his other senses.

He feared the worst may have happened. A person, a stranger, lay on the other side of the door dead. Unable to rescue him and incapable of raising the alarm.

He sat and postulated about how the end would come. He'd read somewhere that starvation and dehydration were agonizing ways to go as the body slowly ate itself. He sat and considered what would happen and how long it would take.

If it was going to happen, he wanted it to be quick. Yet as he sat, agitated and sore, he knew that he would be there for weeks, slowly losing his capacity to think, to swallow, to move – until the end came.

This is not what he wanted. It was only meant to be a thrill. This was quite agonizing now. If, and it was a big if, but if he made it out he'd never do this again. He couldn't. He wouldn't.

Although if this was all part of their plan...

He had said he wanted his limits tested. Perhaps this was it? Maybe they were stretching his horizons. Maybe they were showing him what was possible. Could it be this was all designed to scare him, to show him that he could be taken to places he never thought possible? Maybe this was meant to be.

Then again, maybe he was going to be left to die. He was unsure what to think, what to feel or to expect. Maybe they'd come back. Maybe they'd... Was that a noise? Was that the bolt... or was it just the pipes again?

THE END

Further titles by Mark Sinclair

I'd Sooner Starve!

THE TROJAN CURSE

By Poppet

Driving through the empty parking lot the rain smears gaudy splashes of bloodletting between ripples of neon green. The kitsch signs vie for dominance with the strobes of forked lightning overhead; the soundtrack of nature has a bass that cracks good intentions and shudders foundations.

I watch her standing under the umbrella as if it were Apollo's shield and she the chosen. Why are women so afraid of a little rain? It might do her the world of liberation to run through it stark naked. It rejuvenates the mind, invigorates the soul, and jolts the flatline of life into beating with an engorged pulse. It reawakens purpose and gratitude.

These policies and regulations whereby we are forced to adhere to societal rules is a load of shit. What you're looking at is dulled dullards. Put them in clothing, cut off their senses from their natural surroundings with shoes and umbrellas, cloak the serenity with endless noise, and let the battle for supremacy be over before we've spilt a drop of anger. When the blinkers are placed on the new-born they never think to look left or right, or defy. What comes naturally is asphyxiated with the very first breath of polluted air, and their freedoms are curtailed the second their naked form is swaddled in a straightjacket and crying wails are silenced with pacifiers.

Mutiny is a sorely missed acquaintance in this world of insipid apathy.

Steam exhales a low froth over the asphalt and the multitude of raindrops sound like a nest of termites eating through rotten wood even though the percussion lands on cheap rusting tin.

The challenge steps into the awaiting door of the limo, nary getting her coat moist. Coddled and cosseted to the point of living in a capsule of sensory deprivation.

"Are you sure she's the target?" asks Darren, while exhaling his cigarette smoke.

The pattering of rain hardens to the tempo of a cabaret in full swing and I continue pickling the Toyota out of the parking lot as if we conveniently used it as a short cut at the exact moment that long legged precocious package joined the elite cargo inside the extended vehicle ahead. We're slipping shadows in a midnight of nightmares writhing their wet bellies across the saturated stench of petrified bitumen.

"Positive mate."

Rain mists the ground, road steam dances in the headlights while the putrid smell of rancid oil from the fast food joints stain greasy smears on the anointed tar. The ground is puddled gloss which smells of petrol and coagulated filth now that thunder has come to shake the dead from their silent trance.

Next door is the cemetery and I know that's where she's headed. Where else would you expect to hide seven virgins? Where else would you expect to find their cloning facility? It's the perfect ruse. The failures go directly into freshly dug plots and no one thinks to audit the reams of tombstones poking out of the ground the way razor clams protrude after tide.

Ripe for plucking, picking, digging, and sucking.

God sucking. Hell yes! I've had plenty of missions in my lifetime and none have promised the succulence and debauchery this one does.

Darren looks at me, the distaste still evident, saying gruffly, "When you said we was robbing a bank I didn't expect it to be a sperm bank. This is messed up, Bob."

"It's the perfect assault. Trust the guv, he knows what he's doing."

"But why? She seems harmless," he argues. "Except for maybe drowning in wealth I can see no reason ta'do this."

"The queen bee rules the hive. Take out the elite seven and we're sorted. Ye can't see it Darren, but this uprising has been growing for thousands of years. We have to halt it before it gets out of hand. Before they outnumber us."

"What's the fucking threat?" he snarls, twisting his bulk to stare hatred through the gloomy interior.

His face is eerily painted by the weak fog lights as we maintain a sedate pace behind the precious cargo ahead.

"Wait 'til you see the facility. Shut your gob until ye have all the facts, yeah?"

Parking down at the soot blackened mausoleum I watch the limo through the binoculars, satisfied when it goes under the funeral home, the iron door rolling down in a grating rumble which is overpowered by another grumble of thunder.

"Right, she's in." I dive into the back, grabbing the canisters of milk. "We have exactly five minutes to get this into their water supply if we're to keep to their purification ritual."

He grunts something unintelligible at me before hauling ass, hefting the canisters onto his back, both of us grabbing our tools and hightailing it to the pipeline to the right of the facility.

Climbing down the manhole I switch my headlamp on, following the map drawn in permanent ink on my hand. It's easier than fannying about with paper and chit.

Darren's sweating in the fetid dank, and mutters, "Why milk fer fuck's sake? Milk never harmed a fucking thing. Anthrax maybe, yeah, but not this shite."

"Lactation is anathema to them. We need them out for thirty-six hours for this to work, and milk does that. Now will ye fucking cut the crap and get on with it? Get to the boiler room and I'll take the freshwater supply."

Splitting up, I find the well, dumping litres of fresh cow's milk into it. This had better fucking work. If I wasn't so bloody sure of Godrick I'd think he was taking the piss.

Moving to the reservoir which feeds their taps I deplete my supply, leaving the canisters behind. Shimmying back down the sewer I move to Darren's location, sitting down and starting the timer. We have a long wait to endure while they bathe in the waters of the vestal goddess. Fucking weird cult. Their time has come and it will be my pleasure to take twenty for the team. Even have a nice stash of V in case performance anxiety knackers my pistol.

The pressure release of his final canister spurting into their hot water supply fills me with a weird sense of elation. A cult of virgins and we're sent to deflower them. Fuck man, there's a god after all.

He sits next to me, his reccie build imposing in such a confined space, "Why thirty-six hours?"

"They're not stupid, Darren. They surely know of the morning after pill. We need to ensure the injections take, adhere, they have to be fertilised or we fail our mission."

"Who gets the queen?"

Smirking in the red glow from the heated pipes simmering forge hot, I dig in my pocket, "I'll flip ye fer her."

Steam vents, coating the walls with more condensation, weeping for the foul about to befall the damsels of Taurus.

They worship the bull, they are the seven sisters, the seven virgins keeping themselves chaste. What they could never know is they're all about to become the virgin Mary's kindred. Virgin births will be imminent. Godrick said they gestate faster than humans, they'll be balloons in two weeks, our mission almost accomplished. I can't fucking wait!

Flipping the pence, I snap, "Call it."

"Heads." He laughs at his wit.

Catching it and slapping it onto the back of my left hand, I look at the coin. "Fuck."

"With pleasure," he grins, seeing he won the greatest prize of them all.

Arsewipe.

Twenty hours later we crawl out of our hole, taking the ducts to the inner cavity of the cult's domain. We both have backpacks crammed with ice packs and specimens. It's heavy and it's gonna be weird, but I don't rightly give a shit.

Slowly bending the fiberscope I check the ladies baths. The seven are all passed out, perfectly naked and perfectly prone. They have no security in here which is a fucking bonus of epic proportions.

"Time to get to work mate," I whisper to Darren behind me, unhinging the grate and bashing out the hold of the puerile screws.

Dropping down from the ceiling I roll, pointing at my quarry, indicating he take the other three.

He smirks, that cut-throat, razor sharp, thin lipped cusp of danger which indicates murder is imminent.

I've seen that look too many times to trust the man. He'd cut me down in my sleep if someone offered the right price.

Unzipping, I examine the woman splayed on the marble in sacrifice. One step for mankind. The war is on.

No condoms, blood for evidence, take a photo of every conquest. I get to it, finding the act dissatisfying without a scream, without the struggle, a whole lot of fuck all for my ego except the knowledge that I'm the first in this tight pussy, and will likely be the last.

Darren's grunts are animalistic and I move to vestal virgin number two while the big boy goes wild on the unconscious damsel. I bet he digs snuff films.

It's hard to concentrate with all the fucking noise he's making and I pop a blue, knowing we have to personally violate these seven to get the fat paycheque.

iPhones snap bright flashes as we capture the proof for Godrick, working our way through the few in here, the perfect chaste who clone Amazons in their underground facility. They've been assembling an army for years, readying for assault on mankind by the feminine underground. The cult has grown vastly over the past five years. Congress has fucked it up going public with our agenda, own the uterus and you own the nation.

It sent women into overdrive, ready to fight for their rights as 'human beings'. Equal rights. Not on my fucking watch, pretty.

Ire reawakens a flagging libido and I nail bitch number four, satisfied we've done our duty for God-rick.

Adrenaline is keeping me hyper and I'm almost on a giggly high when he zips up, both of us removing the rings of the brotherhood, heating them up with our lighters. Then we brand our virgins as being God's property, singeing their left breasts with the sigil of the crucifix.

Vigilant, I gesture we maintain silence as we go down to the lower levels. They have a definite routine, all of them should have bathed or consumed contaminated water by the time we get down there. No one should be lucid or able to defend themselves.

He nods, shouldering the harness of our mobile sperm bank, taking the stairs to sublevel Maia. Sneaking out, he goes left while I go right, our coms at the ready and our guns ready to plough down any of these fucking abominations.

"All clear," crackles gruffly in my ear.

"All clear," I mimic, staring at the warehouse of cots with women fiercer than the Governator laid out in comatose perfection.

Starting at the end, I get out the syringe, sucking sperm into the vacuum, sticking it in and expelling it as fast as I can. Fuck we have our work cut out for us. A few more men wouldn't have gone amiss on such a vast mission.

"Bob," crackles in my earpiece.

"Wha'?"

"Isn't this sabotaging our own agenda?" asks Darren, from his side of the compound.

"How d'ye figure that?" I snap, giving this one with a landing strip a bit of a finger, sniffing it like a Cuban cigar before plunging the syringe in there to impregnate the warrior.

"We're doubling their army, mate."

"You're a dickwad, Darren. Can ye not think ahead?"

"Yeah? Fuck you Bob!"

Pausing to refill the syringe, I smile at the fallen. They never saw this coming.

I have a wee guffaw at that.

"Darren, it's right simple. A pregnant woman can't fight. Once they have their own flesh and blood we have ourselves the perfect hostage situation."

"Yeah?" crackles in my ear, and I curse cos I just lost count of how many I have left to inseminate.

"The Trojan war is old news dude. We infiltrate them from the inside. We weaken the organism, it makes their bones fragile while the babe leeches minerals from their bones, childbirth leaves them weak and easy prey, and it costs us nothing but a hard-on."

"Oh yeah," he mutters, sounding impressed.

"They will still be fertile, their fertility is their weakness. We repeat this process the week the spawn are born. They'll fall pregnant immediately because they're fucking flawed that way. They'll be so fucked after a year of this we'll have broken them open from the inside, literally. This is a war, Darren. When women think they can tell us what the fuck to do and how often, a little left and a little right, and do the fucking dishes, and all that fuck, they messed with the wrong effin species! We don't form a bond to the offspring, we didnae grow it inside us right? What the fuck do we care? There's a reason why soldiers have to impregnate the women of their enemies. Take one for the fucking team and we keep control."

"The Trojan curse." He laughs in my ear, "It's an inherent weakness in their organism. The battle starts with the oldest gun. I fucking didn't get it 'til now."

"Amen brother. Now repeat after me, pregnant women can't fight."

"And that's what makes us the stronger gender. And we're here to remind them lest they ferget," he crows. "Plant the enemy inside the gates, then break the gates wide open. Fuck!"

Amen Godrick. The Trojan curse will prevail. It always has and it always will.

Rise up against us and we'll rise up against you the old fashioned way. Nothing destroys a woman faster than her child shot in the eye. We just have to destroy a quarter of the new-borns and they'll never rise up against us again. They're breeding machines. We lose nothing, they lose everything, including their ability to fight.

The bonus is, we're breeding a new army for ourselves.

"Long live Trojan warfare!" he bellows clearly completing his mission. Just in time too cos so have I.

"They're the Trojan horse, all of them, all we have tae do is hide a wee little gift inside the walls and wait for them to destroy themselves. Simple right? It was always simple."

Chucking the empty containers back in the satchel, I hook it onto my shoulder, tempted to write across the wall...

Pregnant women can't fight. Consider yourselves fucked.

THE END

Further titles by Poppet

Darkroom
Satanarium (Darkroom Saga Book 2)
Over Exposure (Darkroom Saga Book 3)
Wrapture (Darkroom Saga Book 4)
Quislings
Dusan
Penance

Wild Wolf Publishing

Fiction ... with TEETH.

www.wildwolfpublishing.com

www.ingramcontent.com/pod-product-compliance
Lightning Source LLC
Chambersburg PA
CBHW070938250626
47159CB00009B/3305

* 9 7 8 1 9 0 7 9 5 4 2 4 5 *